WAR THUG 2

HUGO NAVIKOV

SEVERED PRESS
HOBART TASMANIA

WAR THUG

Copyright © 2016 by Severed Press

WWW.SEVEREDPRESS.COM

ISBN: 978-1-925493-38-2

1

Terra. That's what we in the Space Navy were trained to call Earth from the very beginning of the War on Alien Aggression, to loosen our ties to a mother planet we were unlikely ever to see again even as we fought to protect her. At the time of my birth twenty-eight years ago, when I still called the planet "Earth," 2.5 billion humans lived on its surface. Thirty years before that, over 10 billion people were alive and well. They were totally unaware that death was about to rain from the skies in an alien invasion so shocking, so devastating, that 75 percent of the world's population would die in less than three months.

Humans had been to other solar systems by the time I was born. We were searching for what are still called "rare Earth materials" (even though they are just used up, not rare—humans having mined every ounce of them from Terra, making them now "rare off-Earth materials"). Things like the lanthanides and yttrium used for technology that had kept civilization on Earth running for 150 years, ores and compounds for which we had no substitutes. Thus, to keep our civilization running smoothly, trillions were spent to go in search of these necessities and to discover new sources of mineral riches for our planet.

That's when we discovered extraterrestrial life. Space travelers had run across alien races several times just at Terra's point on a long arm of the Milky Way, epochal events for humankind. Some were intelligent and as advanced or more advanced than humans (these we called "sentients"), and some were just animal-type creatures we called "bugs," because they always seemed to infest any planet they were on, just like insects, with no technology to speak of. (Also, many of them had exoskeletons or chitinous shells and looked exactly like giant bugs.) We were ordered to eliminate them to prevent any chance of them evolving into war-hungry sentients.

Our intentions, then, as I was taught in military school— actually, for decades it's just been called "school"—were purely scientific and peaceful. Humans engaged in limited commerce, and shared scientific knowledge once we and the aliens developed a pidgin language.

To those who could comprehend it, our travelers explained how we could zip through the vast emptiness of the universe through the use of "subspace." Theorized long before a mechanism was found to exploit this loophole in the structure of space, subspace was how the curves of relativistic spacetime could be shot through in straight lines from point to point in our galaxy, like a bullet shot through rolling ocean waves takes a shorter path than climbing the waves and going back down each one. Electromagnetic transmissions could also be sent through subspace, meaning communications with Earth even from distant systems suffered no more time lag than if the crews were transmitting from Mars. Civilian survey crews, scientific expeditions, and mining operations were, just before the attack, the most common missions. But coming in at a close second were privateers, doing what pirates have always done—plundering, kidnapping, anything they could get away with.

A watershed day in human history was when a crew of scientists explained to the leaders of a technologically advanced, spacefaring race of Xenos how subspace worked and could be accessed, and they were astounded. They had hundreds, maybe thousands, of spaceships in their Armada, and we knew they frequently used the armed vessels in skirmishes with other civilizations in their system and one three light-years away. Their scientists were overjoyed that (I'm using Earth-time measurements here) this fifteen-year voyage could now be made in less than one. We explained how we had arrived at their system in just over a month, even though most of a human lifetime would have been required to go that far traveling through normal Minkowski spacetime.

Then we showed them exactly what star in the sky we had come from.

This was a mistake.

Less than a year after this scientific crew's departure from the exoplanet, the Armada of the Xenos—their actual species' name and planet's system has been erased from history books and forbidden ever to be spoken—arrived in Earth orbit and began an attack on population centers before most humans were even aware we had visitors. Particle-beam weapons, proton bombs, repeated blasts on the moon calculated to rain state-sized meteors onto the Earth, and more still—it was a constant, apocalyptic barrage on humanity, killing almost everyone on our whole planet.

A War Council was formed. In fact, this was the genesis of *the* War Council, which now represented every citizen of Earth whether such representation was wanted or not, and it managed to squeeze three medium-sized ships through the alien Armada and its attacks. Those three craft—the *Pinta*, the *Niña*, and the *Bloody Maria*—were packed full, inside and out, with every advanced weapon and prototype of advanced weapon the Council could seize or develop quickly through its complete control over the government and the military.

One weapon, the "Super-Nuke," had never been tested or even built before, because to set it off on or even near Earth would be (or so the theory said) to burn off every mountain, hill, building, and living thing on the planet, leaving nothing but a sterilized, smoking husk. The theorists who had conceived of the project had never released their findings because they believed it was too dangerous. It was only after the Xenos had killed nearly half of the people on Earth that the right scientists were able to get the plans to the right people within the War Council. The effort to build this weapon made the Manhattan Project look like a group of Amish farmers raising a barn.

And that was only *one* of the weapons packed into and onto the ships of the hatefully (yet hopefully) named "Columbian Extirpation." The trio launched amidst a collection of traditional missiles to obscure their track from the alien ships, then slipped into subspace even before they cleared the moon, an unprecedentedly risky move but the only one that could let them escape unnoticed.

Even in subspace, a craft can travel at faster or slower speeds. Unlike what would be needed to travel through a "wormhole" or even keep it open for longer than a nanosecond, travel through subspace requires no extra power once the initial MacGuffin Pulse is fired. Thus, fuel can be used for faster travel or conserved for later contingencies.

The Columbian Extirpation ships carried a *lot* of fuel. They accelerated until there was just a wisp of vapor left in their tanks, just enough so that once they came out of subspace the *Pinta* and the *Niña* could aim at the alien planet and fly right into it, guns and everything else blazing.

It was a suicide mission, eight patriotic men and women giving up their lives to save the fraction of humankind left alive. Immediately upon slipping back into normal spacetime, everything was shot from the ships that could be shot, with the Super-Nukes kept on board detonating on contact with the alien planet's atmosphere.

They worked. It all worked. Every living thing—no, *every single thing*—on that planet was reduced to cinders. The explosions rocked the planet's inhabited moons out of orbit, their populations doomed to either crash into the planet or be lost forever in the cold wastes of space.

However, there was more to do, and the *Bloody Maria* stayed behind, in orbit around the dead world, armed now only with its Super-Nuke. The War Council made an educated guess, and it was exactly right.

That guess was that, as soon as subspace transmissions from their home world were cut off, suddenly and completely, the Xenos would know we had struck back. It took just days for the entire Armada to leave off its attack. The bastards must not have believed it at first, but reality set in very quickly; they called their ground troops back to the ships and vanished into subspace en masse to put down this counterattack.

However long it took them to retrace their steps back through subspace to their home planet, however much fuel they burned in order to shrink the travel time down from a month to a week, maybe a day—they arrived to find the utter transfiguration of their once-blue planet into a brown deathworld, its surface obscured by the dust and smoke that now constituted its atmosphere.

There was still one Earth spaceship orbiting the dead planet, however, and the crew of the *Bloody Maria* waited patiently until they were sure the entire Xeno Armada had returned. Then, using the fumes of fuel in the ship's engine, they yanked themselves out of orbit and flew straight into the center of the aliens' mass of black dreadnaughts.

And ignited their Super-Nuke.

Thus began the War on Alien Aggression, with the War Council taking complete control of Earth's global (or what was left of it) military-industrial complex. As it looked out unilaterally for the best interests of the remainder of humankind, the Council focused most of the planet's industrial capacity and scientific genius on building spacecraft meant to travel long, *long* distances through subspace. Spacefaring arms of the military were created, Space Navy and Space Army, both of which subsumed elements of the Marines and the Air Force into their missions.

The War Council back on Earth held political and military supremacy since before any of us on the *Blue Celeste* were even born. In the general populace, to disagree with the Council's policies or plans or anything else made one an enemy of the state. If summary execution or transportation as fresh meat to a mining colony or as a "comfort patriot" sex slave on a resort planet could be avoided, the best such an enemy could hope for would be forty-eight unpaid "community service" hours per week digging ditches or, a generation after the attack, collecting the rubble of entire cities to be vaporized. This was in addition to the mandatory paid forty-eight hours of work each week doing whatever it was that the Council deemed worth doing.

That was for the general populace. For anyone in any part of the War Council military, disagreement or protest was considered traitorous, and many an entire ship's contingent had been publicly executed for the speech or actions of a single crew member. *This is a time of war*, the Council reminded citizens daily, if not hourly, *and we are winning the fight*.

The War on Alien Aggression, now in its sixth decade, was being won by the human race by the wholesale genocide of off-worlds' inhabitants. The Space Navy hunted Xeno bugs to extinction to teach them a lesson about potential evolution, but our real target was planets with sentient life, specifically any intelligent beings that were capable *or could at ANY time in the future become capable* of creating advanced weapons or that had mastered spaceflight *or could possibly do so in the future.* This flexibility made our charter as Space Navy SEALs (Space-Earth Aggression Leapers, so-called because we "leaped" onto enemy planets from a ship in orbit using an enormous cord known as a "space elevator") to kill any and every kind of exobiological life and secure all technology discovered for future retrieval and reverse engineering by the Council's science teams. We killed, we planted a beacon for those teams, and then we moved on to our next assignment, which could come in a day, a week, or even a month.

This was why "resort planets" were so important to the war effort—not only as punishment for enemies of the state as but vital recharging opportunities for soldiers and sailors. They also were hubs for all kinds of intersystem commerce, so if a soldier wanted to spend his hard-earned credits on something a little stranger than the usual, he could.

This was life under the War Council. And it worked! The war *was* being won—not a single alien attack had followed the original catastrophe—and the less populated this part of the galaxy was, so much the better for continued peace and security on Earth.

Killing was the path to absolute security.

This was all perfect for the *Blue Celeste*, as we Space Navy SEALs were the top of the heap when it came to going anywhere and killing anything at the instructions of the government. We were not brainless automatons—even our infantrymen were top graduates of War Council Academy—but we were sworn under sensory distress and randomized punishment/reward conditioning to do *exactly* as we were told, *exactly* when we were told. The objectives of a mission were known to none of us except our platoon commander, whom we called "Sarge" in person and "War Thug" when we were alone, and even he got only the pieces of the puzzle that we needed to do our jobs. Sarge had always carried out the Council's orders using his own strategies and experience, and the crew of thirteen as we had been constituted for four years had never failed to execute orders and had never lost a trooper.

But then came Planet Bunghole, a mission which went sideways almost as soon as our boots touched the ground. As I relayed in an earlier mission log, we thought we were being sent to rescue three scientists under attack from Xenos … but really we were sent there as a unit to be experimented on and turned into super-soldiers who would be less human than some alien races we had encountered (and killed, obviously). We had done our jobs perfectly, but the War Council marked us for genetic alteration (again—the first time being when we received our Enhancements) and irradiation, and once we were "complete," we would be set upon one another in fights to the death to see who survived, and then the whole show would start again with the arrival of a new ship of SEALs coming to "rescue" the scientists. Our misery and horror would become data points. Our service meant nothing to the powers of Terra beyond the idea that our excellence could mean even better mindless mutant fighters.

We were betrayed by the War Council.

Whoever is reading this log may not understand what a mind-twister this represented to a platoon of Space Navy SEALs. We soldiers of the War on Alien Aggression could by definition *not* be betrayed by the War Council, because our mission was to execute whatever orders we were given, including suicide missions or (in this case) even worse. To do otherwise was treason, rebellion, mutiny … and the Council would spend whatever resources it needed to make a very public example of our capture, our torture, and our executions.

So we were on the run.

We had been following orders and wiping out aliens—both sentients and bugs—for so long, for so many missions, that none of us at first could really comprehend the depth of the fecal slush we were wading through. Yes, we as a platoon had just wiped out not only the War Council's pet bioweapon project; but more than that, Sarge set off a Super-Nuke that scoured everything from the face of Planet L-22233—which we grunts designated "Planet Bunghole"—like steel wool on a dirty pan. For only the second time in human history—that we grunts knew about, anyway--a Super-Nuke had been deployed. It had been installed inside Sarge's artificial right forearm, and we as a team had to rip the huge man's robotic prosthetic from the muscles and sinew that had grown into it in order to get Sarge off-world and up to the ship.

7

But we got it, set it to go off, and got the hell out of there, double-time.

We killed Planet Bunghole instead of allowing ourselves to be made into monsters, as *many* platoons before us had been forced to do by the Council before the SEALs even realized what was going on. We directly and purposefully contradicted the orders of our superiors who were trying to vivisect us.

Thus, in the eyes of the all-seeing Council, we were now traitors. We found ourselves on the run without a supply line, anyone to trust outside our ship, or even a safe place to hide out for what was probably going to be the short remainder of our natural lives.

*****

"This is still a military operation, assholes. Doesn't matter if they ain't here yet to take us all to Heavenworth Base," Sarge barked at us when we remained in our bags attached to the bulkhead past what normally would have been reveille. "Get your asses out of bed. We got a lot to discuss before they come for us. Shit, shower, shave—then report in five."

There was, and we did. I'm Boswell, the log keeper, because of my Enhancement of eidetic memory. That means I have a perfect recall of everything that anyone says or does within my ken, anything I read, everything. (That's why my chronicle of our platoon can include what other people said and did in my absence; I remember every word, every gesture, from my later debriefing of them. Maybe an accurate accounting could save us from being sent to the military space prison Sarge mentioned. Maybe not. We'd probably be executed as traitors as soon as the Council found us. But I don't know how *not* to record everything into the ship's log anymore, not after serving so long in deep space with this platoon.) I counted off our platoon in my mind, as I always did, even though Sarge would know if anyone was missing immediately, having held us together and alive through more missions than I could count. (That's technically not accurate: I could remember every one of our eighty-two assignments over the past four years.)

Sarge had given us our handles, in alphabetical order so that he could use the mnemonic to keep track of everyone. I noted each one of my cohorts in the chow hall, dazed but anxious as they floated in and Velcroed themselves into seats around the table or "stood" along the edges of the room. We kept ourselves in place in zero g's by tucking a foot or leg under something bolted down as we shot drops of coffee into their mouths. A headcount:

A was for Ace, our pilot on the *Blue Celeste* and point man in orbit while the rest of us killed every bug on a planet targeted by the War Council, or killed sentients and reported on what potentially hostile technology the Xenos had. (The Council would then send a crew to collect the tech and save Terra from another potential attack.) Her Enhancement was a complete, 100-percent–solid spatial orientation. In other words, she could tell you north from south on a planet better than a compass could, because Ace didn't rely on shifting magnetic poles. She just used her altered genes, specifically attuned for her role in battle. Right now, however, her sleep-heavy face looked like she wouldn't be able to find her way back to the cockpit without a trail of floating breadcrumbs.

B was for Boswell. That's me. I went everywhere with Sarge on every mission, a fighting soldier but one who was often shielded because I was the only reliable record we would have in case of a Council inquiry. If we were caught after the Planet Bunghole treason—and it *was* treason, no matter how morally justified we felt about it, and we *would* in all likelihood be caught—I would be tortured unto death to squeeze every bit of intel out of me. I did not foresee a pretty fate.

C was for Calico. She was an assassin, one of two in our crew. Assassin SEALs were vital to our mission of killing every living thing on a planet, or at least everything we could reach. Mostly they fought with railguns and grenades just like their mates, but they were also tasked with relieving protected Xenos from the burdens of their lives. These might have been military or even some kind of ruling class, but they were kept out of the main battle and needed to be picked off individually by assassins. Calico's Enhancement was her ninja-like skills at concealment and stealth, much like a cat which sticks its claws into your neck without you even realizing it was there.

D was for Dahlia, one of our two dedicated infantrymen. She was the opposite of Calico, built like a reinforced adamantium shithouse, all muscles and bulk. Of course she was also a crack shot and a dedicated killer, but her Enhancement was unbreakability. She could receive an injury and have it healed in minutes, if not seconds. (You may wonder why *all* SEALs weren't given this extremely valuable and useful Enhancement. The reason was that it "healed" any other Enhancements, seeing the manipulation of genetic material as an injury to the body. Most Enhancements didn't play well with others because the War Council's science arm matched soldiers with whatever Enhancement would work best with their existing genetics, but unbreakability trumped all others every time.)

E was for Ernie, our communications specialist. His Enhancement was the ability to receive and transmit any kind of electromagnetic signal, whether intentional messages or the random bleeps and bloops automated electronics gave off as they worked. (We always wondered if the Council could track Ernie by his Enhancement. I guess we would know if it could very soon.)

F was for Fugly, Sarge's ironic nickname for the most beautiful woman—or man, depending on what someone looking upon her found most attractive—any of us had ever seen or ever *could* see. Her Enhancement was called a "glamour," and it made her come across to any sentient being (or hell, to bugs as well) as that being's ideal of beauty, regardless of species or gender (if applicable). She got us in where no normal grunt would even be able to approach, or she provided a major distraction to the aliens we were fighting, "throwing them off their game," as they used to say. Her fighting ability, though, was what we respected, not her Enhancement of appearing inexpressibly beautiful. Also, Sarge had given her standing permission to remove by force the genitals of anyone, member of our platoon or not, giving her a "rape-y" vibe. None of us knew what she "really" looked like, since her glamour was a constant Enhancement, but when she put her helmet and other gear on, she looked just like the rest of us.

G was for Gunner, our weapons man and, naturally, our gunnery sergeant. He was Enhanced with the ability to ignite murderous fury or Zen-like calm in any living thing just by touching it. He used it most often on us, getting us in whichever "zone" we needed for a mission and even during a battle. He also loved to mow down every Xeno he could with weapons he would jack up for his own amusement. This was perhaps ironic, since he was also our unofficial clergy on board, well-versed in the practices of over a hundred different faiths on and off Terra.

H was for Hog, a big ol' farmboy from the nutrition fields of Terra. He wasn't as sharp intellectually as any of the rest of us, but he impressed with his dedication to shielding his mates with his ginormous muscled body if we needed to fix something, put together an impromptu bomb, anything. His armor had taken on all kinds of alien weapons and come out ahead, even though he often suffered bruised ribs and broken bones. He could deal with the pain later, he always told us, and he did. His Enhancement—and to this day I have no idea how this worked—was that he could induce any frequency of vibration into any discrete object. He could shake apart any construct of sentient Xenos, get rid of boulders through one touch, and of course vibrate an alien until it turned to jelly.

I was for Inman, our ordnance and armor expert, not to mention a first-class wiseass. His hearing was Enhanced to the point where he could detect vibrations inside a nebula as sound and tell us what was going on with any alien warships in the cloud. On any planet or moon with even a tenuous atmosphere, he could hear a single footstep miles from his location. (His spacesuits were outfitted with special earholes to let sound in, but not let oxygen out.)

J was for Junebug, our other assassin. Her special assignments were the same as Calico's, but while Calico skulked in the shadows, Junebug's Enhancement—extreme physical density—made her more of a battering ram to get at any protected and important sentients. She just ran like a bat out of hell and let her momentum get her through any kind of door (or wall, actually), where she would usually dispatch the target with her sidearm or rifle. Occasionally she would just crush them to death by leaning on them if they were upright and lying on them if they were prone.

K was for Killshot, our sniper. His Enhancement was super-powered sight. Not only could he see enemies approaching long before any of the rest of us could, he could also take them out at the very edge of his rifle's range.

Finally, L was for Leonard. (This was his actual name, but since it fell within Sarge's mnemonic system, he just kept it.) He was our technician, able to repair everything from our hydronium-pellet railguns to broken suction valves in our ship's heads. His Enhancement was bizarre, but it could freak out—not to mention kill—sentients and bugs alike. Leonard had the power to take any amount of electricity, from a tiny spark of static to that in the main cables from a spacecraft's power plant, and magnify it while rerouting the energy however he needed. His entire right arm had been lost in battle, but the metallic automail replacement was as functional as any natural arm and helped conduct and redistribute electricity. He could do it for show, to scare our enemies into surrendering (and whom we then killed, of course), or he could shoot it right through Xenos, their weapons, and their technology if necessary. (The War Council frowned upon the destruction of tecnhology because it wanted to know what was out there that could be used against Terra, but if it constituted the only way to subdue and take out the aliens, the Council allowed it. Complete extinction of any potential threat was its main goal.)

And what about Sarge, War Thug? That is to say, our commander with dark tattoos of the word "War" on one arm and "Thug" on the other? Obviously he didn't need to keep track of himself, and not one soul in that chow hall would forget him during a head count, partly because he was physically much bigger than the rest of us with inhumanly muscled arms and legs, but also because he was in our minds and we in his. He was the sun around whom the rest of us revolved. Without him, we would float off into space, our orbits erased.

"Okay, troops," our sun said in his usual growl, "let's hear what Ernie picked up on subspace chatter."

Ernie had to know this question was coming, but as he unattached himself from the chair and stood, he looked as pale as powdered milk. "Sir, the transmissions have been almost nonstop from the quadrant Council base," he said, and that base was so close that it could receive orders from Terra on the subspace band and execute them almost instantly. "The War Council back on Terra sent recon ships to see if the situation on L-22233 was as FUBAR as their own observations and reports indicated. Apparently, it's even worse than they expected."

"A Super-Nuke will tend to do that," Killshot mumbled.

"Secure that," Sarge said, then asked Ernie, "Any idea what they're planning to do about it?"

Ernie swallowed before speaking further, and that gave us all a chill. "The Council didn't send us to Bunghole because we were *lacking* at our jobs, sir. They sent us there because that's where they sent their best platoons, to make them even better in eliminating the alien menace. After all, there will always be more SEAL platoons."

"They said that on *subspace*?"

"No, on electronic pulse messaging, which I can pick up no problem and then transcribe like Morse Code. Must've been some private document, I guess? Maybe from one Council member to another? Anyway, the order has been sent to find us, take us alive if possible for interrogation and public execution, but if that isn't feasible, destroy our ship—and all of us in it—with extreme prejudice."

Breaths were short and faces were blank around the chow hall as we all took in this confirmation of what we already knew: the War Council considered us traitors ... and, technically, we were. (Or at least mutineers, which was the same to the Council.) We had gone against orders, which we had always followed no matter how dangerous the assignment, to save our own skins and stop the insane experimentation; we had destroyed tens of billions of credits' worth of Council property; and we had no doubt been recorded on cameras and microphones hidden throughout our ship, data which was automatically sent to the War Council for archival each day.

As if reading my mind, Sarge said to our communications man, "Ernie, I need you to locate and disable every War Council spycam and sound recorder on the ship before we continue this discussion. I'd rather the Council base not get wind of our plan of action, at least, not from us. I assume you know where they all are?"

"Oh, yes, I do," Ernie said with a slight smile. "They're really very irritating."

"Go on, then, take your time and get every one. Get back here when you're done so Boswell can get you up to speed."

"Aye, sir," he said and, to our mixture of surprise, amusement, and horror, made a circuit around the chow hall, picking off four cameras and their microphones from the very room we were standing in. "I'll get the rest of them, then roast them all in the drive core."

As he left, Sarge took a hard look at the faces of each trooper in his platoon. "I ain't seeing a lot of quit in these faces."

"*Aye, sir!*" we barked in unison.

"In fact, I'm not seeing *any* quit at all," he continued. "That means you bunch of assholes are a lot dumber than I ever thought, and I always thought you were pretty goddamn dumb."

We were all standing now, keeping ourselves in place by holding onto counter edges and cabinet handles. This was as "at attention" as you could be while weightless.

"What you guys *should* do is turn yourselves in and blame me for *everything*, see if you can't get off with a few years at Heavenworth. You assholes don't have to die."

"Permission to speak freely, sir," Calico said.

"Go."

"You should *secure that shit* … sir," she said, and momentarily looked like she wanted to take advantage of her Enhancement and slink into the shadows. But she recovered quickly: "You're too dumb for the rest of us dummies to leave, sir. I'd rather die with my bare ass against the bulkhead window for the Council to see than to abandon my commander."

From nods to spoken *aye*s, we all threw our lots in with Sarge's and Calico's.

"All right, then," Sarge said with an unmistakable but craggy smile, "Inman, you're the smart one—empty your brain on the table. What should we do while we wait for the Council fighters to arrive and kill us?"

"Sir, I think while we wait for them to kill us, we should go vanish on the closest resort planet and maybe not let them kill us. Altair is just a subspace skip away," Inman said.

Chuckles sounded around the room. We all knew Inman loved him some R&R.

"The Taboo Planet," Dahlia said with a smirk. She had dipped her toes into the hedonistic waters on Altair.

"They like to call it The *Forbidden* Planet. Anyway, yeah, I like a nice rest world, but I am serious, sir—I don't have to tell anybody in this room that you can find, um, *employment* in our very specialties at the cantinas that serve the scum and villainy of space freighters and privateer vessels on the ass-end of the planet."

"You're talking about becoming mercenaries," Fugly said, her expression of distaste showing even through the glamour. "You're talking about elite, patriotic soldiers doing some civilian's dirty work for money."

"No, Fug. I'm talking about *disgraced, traitorous ex-soldiers* doing some civilian's dirty work for money." Inman shook off the affront and said to all of us, "Also, the War Council is usually … well, *hesitant* to storm onto a resort planet."

"That's right—resort worlds get chartered only after banning anything more than a slingshot," Killshot said. And he would know, having spent almost as much time at resorts as his fellow hedonist Inman did, drinking, hallucinating, and making time with the sex slave "comfort patriots." This was the unfortunate humans' life sentence for treason, or they worked at the resort planets at least until they couldn't function anymore. Then, I assume, they were sent to the Ceres or other Terra system mines to work and die, but I had no idea, really. I was a bit ashamed that, as a good soldier all these years, I had never really thought about what happened to them when they could no longer "comfort" anyone.

Calico jokingly whined, "Aw, does that mean I have to stay on the ship while you guys get to party—"

Sarge barked, "This ain't a party, soldier. We're trying to *not* get our asses vaporized by the Council. Uncharted territory, troops, so we got to keep clear heads and make sure we don't get noticed. Inman, spit out what you were getting at or secure your mouth."

"Aye, sir," Inman said, and picked up right where he left off: "The real reason the War Council lets these planets operate relatively hands-off is because even SEALs and the rest of the Space Military will go nuts without a break in the constant killing. But that's not all—they let freighters run between the mining planetoids and the processing sectors and then from processing to construction or whatever to keep healthy the third of the Terran economy that *isn't* spent on war."

"More than that, sir," Killshot added. "This galactic war is expensive as hell, and we've all heard about the *other* businesses unofficially allowed to operate on a resort planet. It isn't just whorehouses and bars and opium dens—the Council is bringing in tons of credits through, shall we say, *non*-military sources."

"What's your sourcing on this?" I asked. I like detailed records for the log. "Killshot? Inman?"

Inman sort of mumbled *A guy told me on Space Station 7*, but Sarge's bark cut off the friend-of-a-friend bullshit: "Your *point*, soldier."

"Aye, sir. A resort planet is the only environment in this sector where you aren't being watched every second. The War Council won't attack a resort planet. They won't invade it or do anything to cause a panic and let anyone think the war is going anything but perfectly. They might send an assassin down who can use her body as a weapon—"

"Damn straight," Calico said quietly to Dahlia, who shared her smile.

"—but that would be to eliminate *one* target, maybe a human arms dealer selling to the Xenos or something. Otherwise, somewhere like Altair is the last place the Council would expect enemies of the state and traitors to run—it's where lots of the *punished* go, so it would be like a criminal trying to hide out in a prison. Also, because of the lucrative trade and vital anti-PTSD environment the planet maintains, it's where the Council would be the most, um, *hesitant* to cause an incident."

Sarge looked over his troops and said, "Well? What do we think, assholes?"

"Don't tell me we're a democracy now," Leonard said with a smile.

"Hell, no," Sarge barked. "I just want to know if anybody's got a better idea."

Everybody looked at everybody else. No one spoke up.

"All right, then," our commander said, and at that moment Ernie came back into the room, a biohazard bag ready for burning in the core, filled with what I assumed were smashed camera, microphone, and tracker parts. "Ernie, we clean?"

"Not totally, sir. I got every transmitter and such on board the ship. But there's still a homing beacon, one that gives the Council our exact position at all times, inside the nose cone of the *Celeste*. It can't be removed from inside."

Sarge chewed his lip. "So we need extravehicular activity? Crawling on the exterior of the ship in our leaping gear?" We had to wear spacesuits when jumping down the space elevator cable from airless space, not to mention when exterminating natives on a planet without a breathable (by humans) atmosphere.

"Aye, sir, but it's not on the front of the cone. It's *inside* it."

Groans sounded throughout the room.

"So what do we do? Scuttle the ship?" Hog asked in all earnestness.

"Naw, nobody's scuttling shit while I'm running this tub," Sarge said, then looked at Leonard, who had the electricity Enhancement. "All we need is to short it out. Think you can run a couple of bolts through the beacon, soldier?"

Leonard, who was Black back when attention was paid to such things, nodded but looked almost green.

"Problem? Tell us now or buck up, trooper."

Leonard cleared his throat and said a bit weakly, "I've only done simulated EVAs. I mean, except for leaping while clipped to the elevator. But never just … *in space*."

"Well, we'll have magnets that keep us clamped to the hull," Sarge said.

"Excuse me for pointing this out, sir, but I can't be near a powerful magnet when I use my Enhancement. A strong magnetic field would bend the electric field out of shape in unpredictable ways. It could shoot the lightning right through the magnets—and bodies—in the suits of anyone within a couple of meters of me, or might send the charge all the way through the ship and fry everything electronic inside."

"That would be fatally inconvenient," Junebug murmured.

"Is she right, Leonard? Is that a no-go, then? I'll have plenty for all of us to do on the EVA, so maybe I could assign you to something—"

"No, sir! I will do it myself. I just have to do it without magnets. I have to do it like I'm rock climbing, using handholds like rivets and warning lights. As long as I can get to the nose cone, it'll take literally two seconds for me to burn that homing beacon out." Leonard spoke like a true SEAL, even though he looked like he really wanted to vomit, and in zero g's that is ill-advised, indeed.

Something hit me, and I spoke up: "Wait—Sarge, what else do we need an EVA for? It should only take one person to disable the beacon."

"You can't take weapons onto a resort planet, remember?"

Of course I remembered; that's what I did. I nodded.

"Well, the exterior of our home away from home here is loaded with the finest goddamn killing gear in the service installed in three locations, two up front and one aft. All that shit needs to come off before we land."

"*Land*?" Ace blurted, missing the droplet of coffee she had launched toward her mouth. "Excuse me, but—land, sir? The ship hasn't been landed since she was christened. I'll have to check the manual to even see *how* to land." She was joking, but not by much.

"Then get checking. We're taking all the weapons out of the interior of the *Celeste* as well as off the hull. We're going to Altair without a single popgun. All hands prepare for EVA—except those of us who need to study up on how to land a spaceship." Ace actually reddened at this, but the rest of us listened closely. "I want all the pistols, railguns, whatever the hell you assassins use, *everything* neatly by the airlock. Ace?"

"Sir?"

"How long to make the subspace jump to Altair?"

Our pilot checked a chart on the vidscreen nearest her. "At a good speed, less than an hour."

"Can you get us there in fifteen minutes?"

Ace didn't laugh, but she did look damned surprised. "If you don't care how much fuel we burn, then yes, sir."

"Burn away. Chances are, we'll be meeting our Waterloo there anyway, and it don't take much fuel to get blown to bits." He took in our dejected expressions and said, "Buck up, platoon—rotten luck is a SEAL's bread and butter. If the odds look good, that's when you're FUBAR. So hell, we'll survive long enough to piss off the Council even more. That's a mission worth taking on, if you assholes ask me."

"*Aye, sir!*" we called back, suitably inspired by the chance to make mischief targeted at the very people who wanted to microwave us into monsters on Planet Bunghole.

"All right, then. Ace, pedal to the metal to the Syphilis System. The rest of you, get the weapons rounded up and meet at the airlock in your leap gear in ten. *Go.*"

***

Fortunately for us grunts, it was easy to move even large masses in zero gravity. In two teams of four and one of three, we got every weapon that could possibly agitate the keepers of Altair to the airlock, binding them together with inelastic cord so they floated as several large cubes of deadly technology. Our one-armed commander was at the airlock in nine minutes, in the custom leapsuit designed to accommodate his muscled bulk.

"Sir," I said with a bit of hesitation as I looked at where his automail forearm used to be, "are you sure it's a good idea for you to EVA in … in your, um, condition?"

I spent most days in the company of our commander, since I was the log keeper and general eyes and ears for our mission when information needed retrieval *now*. Even in the time between missions, whether we were sailing through subspace toward a farther system to check it for potential hostiles or spending time at one of the many resort planets that Inman and Killshot were so fond of, I was rarely more than ten yards from Sarge.

That being said, never before had I received a look from him that was what our targets must have seen when he was in "War Thug" mode, that look that made them quiver in place even if they had no knowledge of human physiology. They couldn't know what his expression even *meant*, but their intuition told them it was something very serious, indeed.

Now, looking into those angry eyes myself for the first time, I agreed with them completely. I didn't really recognize the War Thug in front of me as my trusted leader and friend. My mouth opened and closed, but nothing came out.

"Lieutenant Boswell, do I seem *less* to you now that my automail arm is missing? Is my command in doubt because of my *condition*? Speak freely, sailor."

Oh, hell. When he called us "sailor" instead of soldier, we were definitely *not* on Sarge's good side. And he definitely didn't seem *less* in any way.

"I said, SPEAK!"

I automatically sprang to full attention, hands at my sides as during an inspection, and the fact that this left me floating like I was doing an extremely slow somersault mattered to no one. I could see my mates watching this exchange in disbelief—I was always ribbed for being Sarge's shadow and had never been called out like this.

I spoke crisply: "Sir! I was just concerned that it would be difficult to EVA with one hand. It was in no way a challenge or questioning of your authority. Sir."

"I see," War Thug said, his face softening back into our "Sarge" in a way I can neither describe nor, to be honest, comprehend to this day. But it happened, and I was almost tearfully glad it did. "Boz, I appreciate your concern. If we make it down to Altair without the Council finding us and blowing us to atoms in orbit, new automail will be one of my first priorities. Would that be acceptable?"

"Aye, sir," I said with a tiny bit of irony, since he was now giving me shit ... thank god.

"Good. Leonard, can you get my suit outfitted with the right EVA magnet placed about here?" he asked our technician, indicating where his arm ended below the elbow.

"Won't be a problem, sir."

"Didn't think it would be," Sarge said, then looked around the room. "Are we done here, or did anyone else want to ask the cripple if he can do his job? No? Then get your asses suited up and let's go play outside."

***

It was ironic for so many of us grunts to be anxious about an EVA, since technically we did one every time Ace unspooled the giant space elevator cable and we clamped on to slide down to the surface of whatever rock we were visiting. But our time in the actual vacuum of space was pretty short—we accelerated until we got to the top of the exosphere and then down into the thermosphere. If we were planting our boots on an airless moon or a planet with a non-human-friendly atmosphere, we kept our leaping gear on (Ace would send down the supplementary oxygen packs after we all were set down on the surface). But hunting on even the most arid, atmosphere-free planetoid wasn't the same as doing an EVA, where one missed handhold—hence my anxiety about Sarge—could mean floating away in full sight of the rest of the platoon with none of them able to do a damned thing to help you.

The magnets were vitally important, of course, but you still had to pull them off the hull every time you needed to move, let alone execute whatever task you were out there to do. And Leonard wasn't the only one who had done only simulated EVAs—I had never been outside a ship in an uncontrolled environment, and I was pretty sure that went for our assassins and radioman, too. Sarge figured this as well and told Calico, Ernie, and Dahlia to remain inside the ship (assassins wouldn't be of especial help in extra-grunty grunt work, our radioman could route our communications through his Enhancement from safely inside the ship, and Dahlia's "unbreakability" could mean that something might have gone wrong but she'd healed too fast to notice); they would keep watch for anything threatening, so we who were out on the hull could stay informed.

And yes, it was "we"—Sarge wanted me nearby, not only to assist with removing the ordnance but also to keep the log in my head filled with the relevant facts of our new "mission."

Hog and Fugly and Junebug were infantry (we used Junebug as infantry sometimes even though she was rated as an assassin—her density Enhancement was very useful in knocking down Xenos during a battle) and thus trained almost to death in every FUBAR extreme situation a Space Navy SEAL might possibly ever face. They were chomping at the bit to get out there, where they would scamper like king crabs while the rest of us clung on for dear life. *Space* was the enemy here, and they would fight it.

Ace wasn't coming on the EVA, either, since she was the pilot and was needed on board in case of any unforeseen contingencies which I, moving with the rest of the gang into the airlock, was damned glad were unforeseen and could therefore be ignored until they happened. With my Enhancement, as soon as I heard of any particular disaster that could befall us, it would remain there in my mind, remembered forever.

So the nine of us—me, Sarge, Hog, Junebug, Leonard (with no magnets at all because of his electricity Enhancement but tethered to the immensity that was Hog), Killshot, Inman, Fugly, and Gunner—stuffed ourselves into the airlock with the bundled weapons from inside, and once the outer hatch slid open, we floated out into the hostile blackness of outer space. Below us was the green and blue of the resort planet, both overpoweringly near and unreachably far away.

"That looks *good*," Inman said.

"Comm check," Sarge growled over the radio. Each of us counted off, and he gave a satisfied grunt. "Leonard and Hog, nose cone; Fugly and Junebug, aft cannon; Killshot and Inman, starboard bow cannon; Boswell and me, portside cannon. Gunner, you're our point man—any questions or urgent observations go to you, and I want you going back and forth between the three removal teams to make sure we're getting this right. So lay it out for us, gunnery sergeant: What's the plan?"

"There's really no established protocol for this, sir—I mean, I can't think that many ships need to strip their weapons while in flight—but we're going to use Aldrin wrenches to separate the weapon from its hull mount, then shut down the fail-safe and power supply." After each point, Gunner looked at each of us in our helmets to make sure we understood. "Once a cannon is fully disconnected from the ship, *gently* both mates will guide the ordnance to just outside the airlock, attach it to the hull with magnets, and *wait*. All personnel will remain attached to the ship with their suit magnets and teams to each other with tether cables. Everybody with me so far?"

He scanned us all again and nodded.

"Great. Now, when all three teams have maneuvered their cannons into place, we'll use these same magnets to make one mass out of the collected weapons and incorporate them into the bundle of all those collected and bound weapons from inside the ship that we just left inside the airlock. At that point, with all hands accounted for, this mass will be *gently* unattached from the hull and floated to stay in this orbit with our own homing signal on it so we can retrieve it after Inman and Killshot get infected with Sirius Syphilis down on the planet."

Laughs came through the comm, along with a playful "Hey!" from Inman.

Sarge gave a single chuckle and said, "Leonard, how are you and Hog getting rid of that nose-cone beacon?"

"Sir, I'm going to be tethered to Hog, who will clamp onto the ship with his suit's hand magnets and the additional ones added to its knees. When I reach the nose of the ship, I will place my hands on both sides of the cone and let 'er rip. That should burn out the beacon and make the ship untrackable by the Council … or anyone else, for that matter. And Hog will keep me from floating away."

Hog added, "My plan is I'm gonna be *really* heavy."

Another laugh rippled through the comm. In a voice much gentler than his usual bark, Sarge said, "Okay, assholes, let's get this *done*. Then we can get down to the surface and do whatever it is we're gonna do to keep ourselves nice and alive, not sitting ducks for the Council goons, all right?"

"*Aye, aye, sir!*"

∗∗∗

I was with Sarge at the portside cannon, but I can give a narrative of what happened with each team because I always debriefed my platoon-mates for inclusion of their information into the ship's log. It hit me that any log I kept would not be getting sent to the War Council via Ernie transmitting through subspace—in fact, even keeping a log of our continued treasonous activities would be nothing but providing damning evidence against us. However, as Sarge reminded us, we were still a military operation and would conduct ourselves the way we had been trained, even if all our efforts came to nothing in the end.

The four teams and Gunner scuttled across the hull of the *Blue Celeste*, everyone to their assigned places, sticking and unsticking their magnets with no wasted motion or effort. I, for one, didn't care for being in the space environment with only my fingers and magnets keeping me from drifting away. There was never any reason to have ion jets or propulsion of any kind added to the leap gear, since it was intended to be worn only for riding the space elevator cable down and then attaching ourselves for the ride back up as Ace reeled in the many miles of carbon nanotube cord. I was tethered to Sarge, of course, but he could lose his single handhold—

No! I couldn't let myself think of what could happen, because that would always be in my mind and could make me just that little extra bit hesitant, a tiny extra touch of instinctual self-preservation, that could doom us all on a mission. I took in and let out a single deep breath, and this centered me enough to get on with my job. Even if the Council would now be spending what would've been my pay on finding me and killing me, I was still a SEAL and would do what my commander—whether in *Sarge* mode or *War Thug* mode—told me to do.

"Chief and Boswell at portside cannon," I said into the comm, and within ten seconds each of the other teams had reported being in place as well.

"Commence," Sarge replied, and handed me the Aldrin wrench, a tool which could quickly detach the enormous pulse cannon from the ship, even though direct and sustained fire from weapons wouldn't so much as make it shake. The only reason it was even separable from the ship was for repair or to replace it with something even more destructive.

I fit the wrench into the star-shaped hole on the hull side of the cannon and twisted it clockwise until it clicked once, then stopped and clicked it counterclockwise once, then reversed again to click twice times, then again three times, then back again five times. Just a short Fibonacci series, but with each successful number in the sequence, the tip of the wrench expanded inside the locking mechanism and took more of a hold. Finally, the successful combination of numbers and movement detached the cannon as if it had never been a part of the ship. Maybe it was because the *Blue Celeste* was in flight while we did this, but the power to the cannon shut off and the fail-safes kicked in as soon as the weapon was removed. That was a nice surprise. Maybe this whole thing would be simpler than we had thought—

Oh, you stupid jinxing asshole, my mind scolded me. *Secure that shit.*

Floating in space at the same velocity of the ship, the cannon was easy to hold in place while Sarge checked in with the other teams. "Port cannon detached. Starboard cannon, report."

"Starboard cannon detached," the voice of Killshot crackled over the comm.

"Aft cannon ready to move," Fugly reported in her voice lovely even over the static.

A few seconds of silence. "Nose cone? Leonard and Hog, report."

It was dead for another five seconds or so, then the comm crackled with Hog saying, "We're having a little bit of trouble with getting Leonard's hands placed right without magnets, sir."

Sarge grunted, "What's a *little bit* of trouble in this situation?"

More radio silence.

"Hog, get your head out of your ass! *Report!*"

"We can't find the right place for the current," Leonard said in a nervous voice.

Crackle. "Sir." It was Ernie. "I'm monitoring the signals coming from the nose cone as they move Leonard around. They're having trouble because … the guidance computer is routed through the nose-cone beacon. You can't short one out without taking both down."

"That's what I meant, sir."

"Ace," Sarge barked, "can you keep us in the proper orbit and land us without that guidance system?"

"Candidly, sir, I don't know what will happen to the ship if that's nonoperational. I might have full control still, using the stick and referencing the other ship sensors. Or I could have partial control, enough to land. Or we might drop like a stone."

"Our orbit's gonna decay that fast?"

"It's not that, sir. The ship may be programmed to dive out of orbit and straight down toward the planet if the guidance is lost, assuming she must have been blasted at from the front. Without the guidance system, I won't be able to reestablish a level trajectory to get back into orbit. Hell, I won't even be able to pull us out of a beeline straight at the surface."

"So make an educated guess, pilot—what do you *think* is gonna happen?"

"There just isn't enough information, sir. I can't—"

In space, you can't hear anything that your comm doesn't relay, but we could still see, and what we saw was a bright flash from the bow of the ship and an instant of blue lightning sparks shooting into space. Sarge's response was immediate: "*All hands, release the cannons and apply magnets to the hull*—" I had no way of knowing how much of his command was lost to static for the others, but that was all I heard before we started spinning.

I had just released the magnet holding the cannon but hadn't yet stuck it back to the hull of the ship when the *Blue Celeste* swung into an immediate downward spiral. The spin started slowly but whipped us around faster and faster with each 360 degrees we swung around. I just managed to get my magnet secured to the hull before the centrifugal force would have made it impossible for me to move my arm.

The force trying to fling us off (at a tangent of the spinning ship) grew until almost all of our legs were sticking out perpendicularly and the magnets were now the only things holding us to the—

"Oh, *helllllllllllll*!" Leonard shouted into the comm as he was whisked away from the nose cone at last, overcoming the final bit of Hog's magnetic hold on the ship, and we made six more revolutions before their tethered bodies lost velocity sideways and were made invisible by the downward parabola of gravity.

But as the ship wasn't just spinning and it wasn't just falling. In other words, the *Blue Celeste* was hurling downrange as she spun toward the surface. Depending on the direction they were flung to, any of our tethered teams could be *hundreds* of clicks away from any other.

From Hog came only garbled shouts of intense frustration as they fell. We were all wearing our leaping gear, which included parachutes that sensed the density of an atmosphere and deployed at just the right size to slow the descent to g's bearable for a human being but there was no guarantee they would work in a chaotic, non-drop situation. Also, parachutes blooming in the sky of Altair IV would be putting on a very public show in a place where we did *not* want to be noticed.

"Hold is failing!" Fugly was barely able to say, and then she and Junebug whipped off the hull and were sent sailing, tethered together, out and down toward Altair.

Inman and Killshot yelled the same word at the same time, an epithet so foul that the War Council forbade its use in log reports ten years ago. But they both screamed it at the top of their lungs as the centrifugal force created by the spiraling ship overcame their magnets as well, throwing them off in a random direction an undetermined number of clicks from the other two teams.

"Gunner?" Sarge managed to call over the comm, which was failing now as well, probably because our Enhanced communications man was unconscious inside the ship. "Report, gunnery sergeant!"

Gunner didn't respond. He hadn't been tethered to anyone because he was going to be checking on each team as it removed and then bundled together the heavy cannons to float in a stable orbit. He could have been whipped off the hull at any time since it started spinning. And that meant he now could be falling to hit anywhere on the surface of the resort planet, including the open water of Altair IV's two small oceans.

"Goddamnit, Boswell," Sarge muttered just as our magnets lost contact with the ship and we were hurled at great velocity into the atmosphere. I was using my SEAL training to keep myself from a panic attack, but I know I let out shouts and screams as I felt myself launched sideways into the luminiferous aether. But our leap chutes opened at the right altitude and at the right size for a tandem team. We endured the inertial force of our descent being suddenly slowed, but I could see no recognizable structure on this part of the resort planet.

Except for a technically "landed" but still-smoking *Blue Celeste* within view of where we were going to touch down.

"Agreed, sir," I said as I saw Sarge register what was in a heap below us. "Goddamnit."

***

We touched down in a dusty valley ringed by dun-colored mountains, our tether actually helping us not to overreach and trip up once the parachutes delivered us onto the ground. Sarge barely had his chute stripped off when he swept off his helmet and threw it to the side, running for the damaged ship. I ran right behind him, shedding my leap gear as we double-timed to the *Blue Celeste*— and, inside it, Ace, Calico, Ernie, and Dahlia.

It didn't seem to inconvenience Sarge that he was missing the lower half of his right arm—he got to the ship and jumped into the open airlock, then ripped the inner door off with one bare hand and one stump jammed in like a crowbar. The inner airlock door was thrown out onto the dirt and Sarge disappeared inside. I ran as fast as I could to catch up to him, but I wasn't even to the airlock when I heard Sarge let out a howl of anger and despair.

I hope to never, ever hear that sound again, as long as I may live. I wish I had never heard it at all, the sound of a father coming home to discover his children are dead and raging and spitting at God for making this horror of a universe.

I slowed enough to step through the airlock holes gingerly, not wanting to interrupt Sarge from his grief. But step in I did, and since the airlock was in the middle of the port side of the ship, I could see all the way through the ship, both fore and aft, by turning my head.

Sarge was in the cockpit, sitting in the jump seat behind the pilot and copilot's seats. His head was down and his eyes were closed. He didn't need to see any more than Ace's flight suit looking like it was rolled into a ball and shoved under the instrument panel in the pilot's footwell. As I approached, I could now see what Sarge saw: the flight suit was intact, but our beloved pilot was smeared like Ace had been strawberry jam inside the squashed-flat packet of her uniform. The centrifugal force must have been equal to a hundred freight trains piled on her chest. Even the weight of *one* freight train was enough to kill, of course, but as the spinning increased, more and more force was piled on, eliminating anything that resembled a living thing.

In the very aft of the ship, Calico was recognizable by the stilettos she kept strapped to her thighs even when traveling through subspace, or sleeping, or using the toilet. Her boots were crushed into a thin leather film against the rear bulkhead. Sarge stood after a moment and walked down the length of the ship, walked right past me without saying a word. Once he took in what I was looking at, what remained of the trooper and assassin, he let out a horrifying wail, a lament that felt like it would shake apart what was left of the ship.

What was left of Ernie was in the radio room—really just his soundproofed quarters. He was pressed so far into the aft-most bulkhead that his jellied remains were cartoonishly outlined in the thick nanosteel. The centrifugal force had pushed him inches into the wall before his pulverized body even turned to liquid.

Sarge didn't wail again, didn't even scream. He just leaned against the bulkhead outside Ernie's quarters, all of the strength sapped from his massively muscled frame. He couldn't even lift his head to meet my reddened eyes.

But where was Dahlia? Her uniform wasn't anywhere to be found, and we checked every quarters, every storage area, anywhere that she might have gotten stuck and then crushed to death against the wall.

There was nothing. Dahlia—even the liquefied remains of our unbreakable infantryman—was not on the *Blue Celeste*. Sarge and I regarded each other with a mix of relief and horrible anticipation.

"Theory?" Sarge said with what I heard as hope. His eyes were no longer wet. He had wailed and screamed for the troops that he let die (in his mind, anyway), and now there was a job to do: *Find Dahlia.* And then find everyone else we could.

I pointed out one completely missing "windshield" back in the cockpit. The other was intact. "Sir, I think she might have been thrown through one of the forward viewports when the ship started spinning out of control. How Ace was positioned, she slipped under the instrument panel and couldn't get out with all those g's pushing against her. Same thing with Calico, who must have been in the aft section. My guess is that the centrifugal force threw Dahlia into the viewport so hard that it lost integrity and shattered, throwing her into space."

"Into space? Not the atmosphere of the planet?"

"I think the centrifugal force would have killed her if she were stuck against the viewport for as long as it took for the ship to enter the atmosphere. She had to be thrown with great centrifugal force against the viewport to overcome its strength"—the *Blue Celeste*'s windows were made of aluminum silicate glass and fused silica glass—"because just pressure against it, constant pressure like someone was pressed up against it, wouldn't be enough to knock out the triple panes, sir. There would have to be a locus of sudden pressure to break that."

"Understood," Sarge said. "What about her Enhancement? Could she survive in space for long enough to enter the atmosphere? I'm thinking that maybe—"

"Pardon me for interrupting, sir, but nothing I've read on our crew's Enhancements, including Dahlia's 'unbreakability,' would make me think she could live without air. Her bones and tissues mend themselves—as you know, sir, please excuse my speaking aloud my train of thought."

"Excused. In fact, continue, Boz. I need to know."

"Aye, sir. As I said, her bones, muscles, even organs heal themselves rapidly after an injury, but of course the soldier must be alive for that healing to take place."

Sarge watched me for the conclusion.

"If she got thrown through the viewport into space, she would be dead within twenty seconds. There wouldn't be any healing for her body to do, because it wouldn't be *injured* as such. Kind of ironically, the injuries she suffered from hitting the front viewport would probably have healed before she … um, *passed away*, sir."

"You're a fine sailor, Boz. You do us proud, even in the valley of the shadow of complete FUBAR."

I allowed myself a small smile. "Thank you, sir. Ace and Calico and Ernie and Dahlia were the best platoon-mates—"

"Whoa there, back it up. We don't know yet if Dahlia is a *were* instead of still being an *is*."

"Technically, no, that is true, but ... I don't see how she could have survived. She wasn't even wearing her jump gear, sir."

Sarge chewed on that. "I wish Gunner was here. I could use some spiritual bullshit right now."

I had never heard him say anything about Gunner's pastoral skills, although he had relied several times on our gunnery sergeant's Enhancement that allowed him to incite fury or restore complete calm just with a skin-to-skin touch. I also had never been present when Sarge lost a trooper. It had been four years and eighty-two missions during which I had been his right-hand man, and we had never lost a soldier except through reassignment or leaving the service altogether. As a commander, he *must* have lost troops in the heat of constant battle, but Ace and Calico and Dahlia and Ernie were the first I had been present for.

Not necessarily Dahlia, I reminded myself. But you don't need to see a body to know someone is dead.

"What now, Sarge?"

He pulled himself out of wherever his head had taken him as he thought about our ship's *de facto* spiritual advisor. He straightened himself, set his jaw back to business mode, and said, "Our Enhanced radioman is dead. Whatever beacons and shit the *Blue Celeste* had on board have been crushed by fifty g's. In other words, we got no way to reach anyone on the comm even if they still have their helmets on. Nobody can tell us if the War Council is coming, because we can't tap into the subspace chatter anymore. We're deaf and dumb. Blind, too, when it comes to knowing what direction to go or what to do once we get there."

I looked around the ship. Everything that wasn't bolted to the deck—and a lot of things that were—had been crushed against whatever bulkhead they were pushed against by the unceasing centrifugal force. I couldn't even differentiate my belongings in the pulp left behind in my quarters. Finally, I got myself together and said to my commander, "That's not a plan, sir."

Sarge looked at me in surprise, but then a smirk lifted part of his face. "Well said, Boz. The first thing I want to do is find Dahlia. I can't give you any logical reason, but I feel our unbreakable mate is—"

"Is what?" a voice called from just inside the airlock.

It was Dahlia.

Sarge's mouth just about dropped to the deck as he took in our infantryman stepping into the remains of the ship.

She looked around for just the few seconds it took to register that her troop-mates on the ship were dead. Not only dead—*erased*, their identities nothing but a memory now. "Oh, holy goddamn son of a bitch *shit*!" she cried, then pulled herself together, eyes still dropping tears. "Excuse me, sir."

Sarge's mouth remained open, his eyes unable to accept what they were seeing, no matter how hard he had argued for the shred of a chance that she had not been killed in the vacuum of space. "Lieutenant, you gotta have one hell of a story to tell us," Sarge said, and hugged—*hugged*—my fellow SEAL, who was so shocked it took her a few seconds to return it to our commander, leaning into his chest to cry some more. He led her out of the ship through the airlock, still holding onto the intensely strong, blocky infantryman, treating her like an actual daughter for just a little while.

***

We walked in the blowing dust of this part of Altair, not seeing much to distinguish this "resort planet" from any other miserable rock in the galaxy. None of us had any idea in which direction we should head, so we just followed the setting sun of this system until it was full dark and we could see lights, artificial lights, making a halo at the horizon to what, based on the longitudinal movement of the heavens, we had decided to call north.

Sarge nodded at the hazy light, which on a planet of the size of Altair would put the light sources at about fifteen clicks from our position. "Could be a whoretown, maybe with casinos, but there's people there no matter what it is, and we need to get lost among *people*," he said. "We'll bivouac here tonight. Everybody get yourself a nice, soft rock."

We settled in as well as we could on the gritty ground, but as SEALs we had all been through rougher nights. At least the temperature was Terra-like, which of course it would be on a resort planet. "So?" I said at last to Dahlia, after a few minutes of watching the trajectories of spacecraft in orbit among the sky full of stars.

"So?" she echoed.

"So, how the hell did you survive? What *happened?*"

She took in a deep breath and let it out. "Just before all hell broke loose, I was at the map table near the cockpit, trying to figure how the Council might come after us—from what direction, maybe how many, thinking what we could possibly do to put their torturing asses as far behind us as possible. I looked through the front viewports at Hog getting Leonard set up to send the juice through the nose-cone beacon, and then there was that huge bolt that blew up the nose cone and sent an EMP all the way through the ship taking everything down with it.

"Ace yells back to us, 'We've lost attitude control! Hold on tight—we're going to start spinning—' and we sure as hell did. Ace in front of me and Calico behind me got pinned against the fore and aft bulkheads, as you ... as you saw." She took a moment, then continued. "I held onto that map table as long as I could. I could feel the tendons and muscles ripping and repairing, ripping and repairing, bones and sinew stretching to the breaking point, then actually breaking, then healing again, again and again and again.

"I never felt such pain in my entire life, Enhancement or no Enhancement. Finally, the table I was hanging onto bent under the force of me holding onto it—that solid metal map table bolted to the deck, Boz—and I got lucky. We were spinning so fast then that I didn't think my Enhancement was gonna save me any further. I don't think my brain being crushed against my skull is something repairable. Maybe it is, I don't know and I don't wanna know. But I let go of the table and went hurling through the cockpit and smashed my face into the very center of the three-pane unbreakable viewport ... and it sure as hell broke. We were enough into the atmosphere that I flew through that window and just passed out from the thin air. If I hadn't been able to hang on as long as I did, I probably would've shot out into space and my eyes would've boiled out of my skull.

"Anyway, I fell the long, long way down to the surface, totally unconscious, I'm sure with every bone in my face broken and my skull cracked in frickin' half. I don't remember anything until I woke up, my broken bones re-laced and whatever organs were smashed back to full functioning. I was in such pain that I just lay there for a while, but when I felt the ship's impact rumble through the ground and saw the column of smoke, I knew it was my duty to get back to the *Blue Celeste* and see what good I could do. You guys just barely beat me to it—you saw there was nothing to do but scream at the Council for all of this shit, *all* of it."

She was finished. "Thank you, Dahlia. It's in the record now," Sarge said, indicating me, "and when we reveille in the morning, we'll have two jobs. First, look at that smoke at three o'clock—could be vapor the way it's in the front of the sunset, but whatever. That looks to me like an industrial operation of some kind."

"I didn't think resort planets were permitted to have factories or other major industry. Altair could lose its charter for allowing that kind of thing. And why would they? The credits they bring in just from the brothels and casinos and bars—"

"You done, Boz?" Sarge interrupted, only slightly amused. "I don't want to cut off your completely uninformed speculation or anything."

Sheepishly, I said, "Aye, sir. Done."

"If that's an industrial operation—*if*—that means a concentration of humans who live on this planet. Humans who are long-term residents would notice or hear before anyone else if something unusual was going down."

"Like a Council ship crashing," Dahlia said.

"*Pre*-cisely."

"Once we gather some intel over there—and Boswell, it doesn't matter what they're manufacturing over there, guns or racing ships or dildos, whatever—I bet we'll be able to find the others and get the hell off this rock."

"The others?" she asked. "Of course, holy hell, the *others!*" I could feel her sit up in a panic.

"At ease, Lieutenant," Sarge said. "We're all SEALs. If there's any way at all for someone to survive open space, crash landings, and hostile environments, our gang will do it."

She lay back down and said quietly, "I just hope they're okay. They could be in god knows what hole right now."

2

"Oh, sweet Jovian Jesus," Killshot moaned in admiration as he entered the vagina of the Altair comfort patriot. "Six-four-oh-one, you are wonderful!"

"Ooh, baby," the sex slave 6401 replied mechanically. "Don't stop."

"You bet I won't!" he said with bravado, paying no attention to the dead eyes and lack of even *faked* passion of the woman unmoving beneath him. "I'm gonna make you scream!"

"Eek. Ooh, baby. Don't stop."

"That wasn't much of a scream."

"Huh?" she said, seeming to look at him for the first time. Her makeup was perfect, even after what must have been most of her twelve-hour shift. She mustn't have sweat one time all day.

"Your scream of pleasure, delight, you know what I mean. Doesn't it feel good?"

Her eyes unfocused again and gazed at the ceiling. "Don't stop. Ooh, baby."

Ah, hell with it, Killshot thought, and began sawing in and out of her again to get this over with.

***

"We don't keep any liquor on the ship," Inman told the balding bartender inside the brothel. "We got to stay sharp. But what the hell—I do believe I'll have another Andorian Ale."

"You all right? I hope you're not going to show up for duty three sails to the solar wind."

Inman pulled a face. "Just gimme the drink, all right? I got issues on my mind, and they're overstaying the hell out of their welcome."

"You kids got it all figured out, don't ya?" the barkeep murmured under his breath, as he fetched Inman's drink. But he didn't know about his customer's hearing Enhancement.

"Hey, I'm no kid—I'm a goddamn Space Navy SEAL!"

"W-What? I didn't say anything, sailor." He put the blue drink with white froth in front of Inman.

"Old man, I heard—" he said, but cut himself off fast. If word got to Altair that the Council was hunting for a mutinous ship of Enhanced SEALs, he might be remembered for that comment. "I didn't hear anything but 'kids.' Sorry, Pops."

"You sure got nicer all of a sudden."

Inman shot the whole glassful down his gullet. "I get nicer the drunker I get. Why don't we work on my personality some more?" He put down a twenty-credit token and added, "How much is another ale?"

"Four credits."

"Keep the change, and keep 'em coming."

The barkeep smiled, and Inman let out a breath he didn't even realize he was holding.

A minute later, a hard clap on his shoulder almost made him release his entire mouthful of ale onto the bar. Killshot's voice came from behind him: "Hey, you lush son of a bitch, have you spent all your time at the bar?"

"Have you spent all your time screwing women who aren't allowed to say no?"

Killshot sat on the stool next to his mate. "That is unkind. I'm a giver—I give pleasure to the unfortunate cum-fart patriots who have to endure lackluster lovemaking before I get to them."

Inman made a derisive snort and motioned to the barkeep for another. The older man stepped over and said, "You might want to slow down, son. Andorian Ale just builds and builds until you can barely breathe. You do *not* want to pass out here, believe me."

"Just gimme another goddamn drink."

"Hell's bells, boy, your personality sure isn't getting any better," the bartender said and went to pour the drink.

"So," Inman said to Killshot, maybe slurring his words a tiny bit, "I assume you're here to wait out your refractory period between erections?"

Killshot made an exaggerated face of shock and offense. "Maybe I just want to spend some time with my best pal before we get arrested and execu—"

"S*hut up, man!*" Inman whisper-yelled. "There's got to be a reward and commendation from the Council for our heads, or will be soon. And we spend forty-eight hours together every shift, so I know you're just sitting here until your little rocket can fly again."

"Well, you're sitting here and drinking whatever the hell that is"—he pointed at the glass of living liquid—"until you pass the hell out, so maybe don't judge me."

"I'll drink to that," Inman said, and did. The room was swimming some, but that was to be expected in a sketchy establishment such as this. He waved a hand at the comfort patriots sitting dejected on chairs along the walls of the room, the topless women and men in their shiny shorts awaiting their next tour of duty. "Go forth and get it out of your system. Literally. Heh."

Killshot was kind enough to laugh at that and said, "Don't mind if I do. Meet you up in the room in a couple hours?"

Inman belched and wiped his mouth with his sleeve. "Sure, why not."

Killshot clapped him on the back again and moved toward the ladies and a smaller number of male sex slaves. He chose one of each, who rose sluggishly to their feet and led the way to an empty "love chamber." He followed them with a bounce in his step, since he was going to have them do each other while he waited for his tumescence to return and he could join in.

Inman swayed on the stool, and he could now feel the buildup of alien intoxicant weighing down his body like three g's were pushing him down in an accelerating ship. He was a SEAL, a man who could hold his liquor … usually …

He didn't even know he was falling until he hit the floor, then just stared at the point where the barstools were bolted down. Then he could feel himself being lifted by two sets of arms and dragged off as the barkeep shook his head ruefully. Then he slipped away into unconsciousness, no longer able to wonder why he was being dragged away, or by whom, or to where.

***

Killshot enjoyed the hell out of watching freaky people getting it on, especially with his Enhanced vision that allowed him to see even the tiniest ripple of flesh, but on the *Blue Celeste*, pornvids were (justifiably) seen as distractions a platoon could not afford. Same thing with his beloved spicy Arrakis cigars—*de fumar* on a spacecraft was *no bueno*—the smoke of which he now held in his mouth to extract every bit of pleasure.

Not that he didn't love being a SEAL, doing his duty and getting to kill lots of things as a sniper … but those days were done, weren't they? The ship was who knew where, their weapons lost, and they were soon to be hunted down by the War Council and an excruciating (and fatal) example made of them. So he would enjoy the living daylights out of his favorite vice before he died.

He did love the many sexportunities on Altair, but it all depressed him a bit as well. Even the couple going through the motions in front of him weren't into it even as much as an actual prostitute would be, because they were prisoners, slaves, doing it because not to do it meant a trip to the Ceres mines, where your chains prevented you from even killing yourself.

So he put that out of his mind as he leaned back in the easy chair in their room at the brothel-hotel and enjoyed the mélange of flavors dancing through his retronasal olfactory system as he watched the sex slaves go at it for his pleasure.

He had barely closed his eyes to isolate in repose the wonders of stranger sex and alien tobacco when—

BOOM BOOM BOOM

—his door shook with the heavy pounding of a big fist probably connected to a disturbingly big individual who observed no social niceties or even resort planet hotel rules.

He gently placed his cigar in the curved depression of the freestanding ashtray, trying not to make a sound.

BOOM BOOM BOOM BOOM BOOM

The blasts of concussion from the other side of the door made the two lovers decouple and hide behind the other side of the bed.

If they're not using a key, he thought as he looked around the small and overly tidy room, *they're not with the hotel. But since they're banging on the door instead of knocking it flat, they're not War Council, either.*

"Just a second! I'm not decent—I got comfort patriots in here—"

"*We got to talk to you, Mister*!" a gorilla yelled through the door. "Your buddy's in trouble!"

We? He didn't like the sound of that. But his *buddy* ... "Inman?"

"Yeah, sure, that's the one."

Well, that *didn't inspire confidence.* Killshot wondered for a moment if Altair had organized crime ... or any crime, for that matter. It wasn't a renegade planet, for god's sake—it was a Council-sanctioned resort! But he did know that shady dealings were done on the planet all the time while the War Council turned a blind eye, too busy fighting aliens to worry about the drug trade or stolen private spaceships.

"I'm a Space Navy SEAL, guy. You don't want to tangle with me. I've had a very bad day." He might have made a mistake in giving his military status—the Council *had* to be looking for him—but maybe it would scare off this goon.

"We don't care if you're the President's official ass-wiper, Mister. Open the goddamn door, or we're gonna be unhappy."

"All right, already. But I warned you," Killshot said, and pushed the button to slide the door open. He took a defensive posture that he tried to make not look like one, but his fists were curled tight and he stood on the balls of his feet, ready to go to town if they were thinking of pulling any rough—

As the door slid up into the wall, two mountainous men in matching "Resort Services" jumpsuits rushed in—the blond one behind the dark-haired one, since they were way too big to fit through the door together.

Like a couple of panicked cats, the naked slaves ran past the heavies into the hallway. The intruders made no move to stop them, in fact didn't even seem to notice them, keeping their eyes fixed on their quarry.

That would be *him*.

Killshot took the offensive, immediately cracking the blond under the chin, a move that made the man's head jerk back but left him standing'. That shot should have broken the big bastard's jaw—and maybe it did, judging by the way it was hanging below the skin—but the blond took just a second to shake off the blow and come at Killshot. Only now, the dark-haired thug came around his partner's side and rammed into Killshot, throwing him off his feet. His back slammed into the scoop chair of the room's small table—a chair that was bolted to the floor. *Holy shit* was all Killshot could think through the sudden excruciation. Now he'd have to fight with a couple of broken ribs. But he was a SEAL; he could play hurt.

Before the big boy could get off of him to cause more damage, Killshot threw his knee up into Dark-hair's jewels, mashing them against the son of a bitch's pelvic bone.

For all the thug reacted, Killshot may just as well have tickled the guy's foot. Something was way off here—besides him getting the hell beat out of him for a reason he couldn't even guess at.

As the blond pushed his cohort out of the way and grabbed Killshot's arm in a position to break every bone in the limb, he gasped, "What are you guys, androids?"

Before Blondie could snap his arm in two, Killshot used the bed to let him launch into the air and flip *behind* the goon, maneuvering his arm around the attacker's in the same hold the man had just been using against Killshot, and didn't hesitate to apply the correct pressure—or maybe a little more than that—to crack his assailant's muscled appendage into a painfully useless hanging slab of meat.

But the huge man didn't even blink. He just brought his other arm around—the one with a big clenched fist at the end—and punched Killshot in the side of the head, making him almost black out. But not quite. He sank to his knees and swayed a bit, but just managed not to fall to the carpet. Seeing the dark-haired tough advancing toward him to unleash some fresh hell, Killshot raised his hands in surrender, something he had never done on any field of battle, any stage of training, anything.

His opponents and enemies there felt pain, however. As a SEAL, he was really good at doling out pain, but that gave him no advantage here. It was only because of his Enhancement that during his beating he had noticed the small bluish scar at the top of each man's spine, right where it met the base of the skull. He knew that scar—their pain signal was blocked before it made it to their brains. They could switch it back on after a fight and get their injuries tended to, but until then, they were effectively immune to feeling any pain. But Killshot had no such switch, and he was already struggling to stay conscious. So he held up his hands and said through the blood in his mouth, "Okay, fellas, I give. So what the hell do you w—"

The dark-haired ape stepped up and kicked him in the face. This time he went all the way down. And stayed there.

* * *

When Inman awoke, his head was pounding. Worse, he couldn't move his hands or feet, since—as he saw when he could finally open his eyes—they were clamped to the armrests and legs of a metal chair. Before he could even speak the round of expletives arising in his mind, he noticed that he was clad in a pair of shiny short pants … and that was all.

So was the topless woman next to him. And the shirtless man in the chair on the other side, his face in his chest like he was sleeping. And all the zombie-looking humans chained to the chairs lining the walls.

Comfort patriots, Inman realized, and tested the clamps by trying to raise his arms and legs. They held him tight. *I'm a comfort patriot*. Panic rose in him, but he tamped it down by observing his breath as it rose and fell, a SEAL technique he was damned glad he knew.

He tried to remember what had happened between him sitting at the bar and him sitting chained to a chair like a sex slave, but it was a total blank.

Not *like* a sex slave. He *was* a comfort patriot now. He must have been found by the War Council and summarily sentenced to a lifetime of joyless screwing, buggery, sadomasochism, anything the visiting, stressed-out soldiers and sailors wanted to burn off their fear and anger.

Inman could see the irony, of course, but why hadn't they just executed him along with the others? He thought of all the take-charge banging he had doled out to a dozen resort planets' contingent of sex slaves, and even though he was never violent or even verbally abusive to them, he knew enough to know he was a rare exception. Bruises and rope burns adorned the bodies of almost all the CPs sitting with him.

He turned to the thirtyish man sitting next to him, one that he noticed had no clamps on his arms or legs nor a thick collar around his neck as Inman had. "I don't think I'm—"

BRRZAP!!!

Inman would have launched himself right out of the chair if he wasn't chained down. Even still, his back convulsed in an arc of agony and his eyes felt they were going to burst. He let out a cry of pain—

BRRRRZAPPP!!!

That one was even stronger—and more painful. *"What the f—"*

BRRRRRRRZZZAAAAAAPPP!!!

Even stronger yet. He squeezed his eyes shut so hard tears formed. He kept his mouth locked closed. Obviously, if he made any significant vocalization, the shocks through his collar would rise in intensity. The CP next to him didn't even flinch or glance at him this entire time. The man's gaze remained somewhere a thousand yards in front of him.

Inman looked to the woman on the other side. She looked at him with sympathy, at least—maybe pity—before she turned away and stared off, too.

Maybe she was a newer sex slave, one who hadn't yet lost hope or been used and abused so many times she had to disconnect from this horrible reality. He'd been with more than a few such men and women in his time in the Space Navy and never noticed anything amiss. They banged him like a champ and even talked with him a little before and after. He guessed now that he had just gotten lucky.

You're an asshole, he spat at himself. *You got lucky, how nice. What about those comfort patriots? Lucky just to get your prick? And how about you? Feeling lucky NOW?*

There was no need to answer himself—not vocally, of course, but not even in his own mind. He shifted his gaze from neck to neck of every other CP within his field of vision. One woman opposite him had a collar like his, but that was it. Everyone else had apparently learned their lesson and didn't make a goddamn sound.

The War Council had summarily sentenced him to be a comfort patriot, and if he wouldn't or couldn't cut it, he would be sent to Ceres, deep in the mines where you couldn't even see the stars. Inman shuddered. That didn't set off the zapper, and for that small mercy he was grateful.

He held back a sob. He was a goddamn SEAL, and he was being conditioned to appreciate just not being tortured for making a sound.

His training had begun.

***

Killshot had been a Space Navy SEAL for tour after tour with all the training that involved. He had been subjected to plunges into icy alien waters and pulled six g's in capsules skipping on Jupiter's atmosphere, where one wrong decision would mean plunging into the crushing clouds to his doom. Before he had received his nickname from War Thug and was just known as [Killshot's real name], he faced his final exam, as it were, of SEAL training. This was to fight—to the death—a known traitor in the War on Alien Aggression. One who had, before her treachery was discovered, also been a SEAL, meaning she had killed another fallen soldier or sailor with her bare hands to pass *her* "final exam."

Yes, his opponent in the arena was a woman. She was shorter than he was, meaning her reach would be shorter, her legs unable to kick out as far, her entire body a disadvantage—

In what seemed an instant, her boot struck him so hard in his muscled abs that he staggered back and fell over his own two feet. He barely had time to register the pain before the same boot came to stomp on his head. He rolled just out of its impact, which he knew would have broken his skull into shards shoved into his brain.

He had to regain his feet, but here she came again, rage and determination on her sharp features, running at the spot he had rolled to, ready to drive a knee into his throat and end him.

But he was trained as a SEAL, too. Facing up, he lifted his torso and legs with his arms and trapped the woman's legs, then spun her around until she was the one in the dirt and he was the one standing. He kicked her in the ribs, then just where the ball and socket of her leg fit into her hip, making her cry out in sudden agony. Like a Rollerball forward running to kick the ball to the other end of the rink, Killshot came at his prone opponent, ready to separate her head from her body with one well-placed swing of his boot.

But, despite her shortness of breath and writhing in pain, she bent forward just as his leg swept through the air where her head had been a second earlier. He overcompensated and she took advantage by grabbing his planted leg and swinging her other hand around to drive its ball directly into the middle of his shin, cracking it so hard that the Council training administrators lining the arena winced at the sound.

Vomit raced up and out of Killshot's mouth even before he did a split, one leg still swinging upward from where it had missed the woman's head and the other still held in place by his opponent. The portion of his leg below the break in his shin stayed upright, but above it bent at a 90-degree angle, sending searing horror through his body of an intensity he had never even dreamed of.

If he lost consciousness, he was as good as dead.

So he used the breath technique that had gotten him through panic and pain during his training—training that he was one dead traitor away from completing—and centered his locus of attention on the pained rise and fall of his chest. He didn't close his eyes, couldn't close them, or he would surely pass out from the pain, and so he saw the woman reaching up to grab his testicles. He would have done the exact same thing to another man if he were where she was at that moment, because no male could not be stopped in his tracks—and made easy to kill with a single blow—by trauma to his orchids.

Before her hand could reach them, however, Killshot shot his own hand down to grab her hand in his. Before he could even consciously feel her bare skin, he *twisted*, transferring the angular momentum of his horribly painful pitch forward up his good leg and down his arm. His opponent's hand didn't just break at the wrist and half a dozen other bones—his entire body weight twisted the woman's hand and ripped it right off her arm.

She screamed and fell to the dirt, holding her stump with her other hand as it fountained blood into the air. Very soon she would be unable to stay conscious, Killshot knew, and then he would be the victor, a full-fledged Space Navy SEAL.

Every muscle screaming—he'd find out later that he had broken his own wrist in the violent wrenching off of his opponent's hand—he crawled the couple of feet between them to finish her off while she could still experience her own demise. As he reached forward to break her neck, she turned her head to look him in the eyes.

She murmured something. It didn't have the tone of a plea for mercy, but Killshot couldn't make out what she was trying to say. He moved closer, his hands in position to snap her spine at the skull, and she murmured the same almost-words again.

"What?" he asked, despite himself. She wouldn't be strong enough to fight him anymore, anyway. "You got something to say, champ?"

Maybe because she was a woman, Killshot allowed her a moment to gather her breath and say what was going to be her last words in this life. She moved her mouth painfully and managed to whisper, "I'm not a traitor."

And the ambitious, callous young man that Killshot was at that age said to the girl about to die at his hand, "Not my problem," and he broke her neck with one vicious jerk of her head.

Exhausted to the point of catatonia and the pain starting to register itself in his brain, the soldier who would be Killshot rolled onto his back and stared at the white sky. There was no applause from the dozen proctors who'd been watching, no cheers from any family, nothing. Just his pain and his hitched breath and the knowledge that he would very soon be helping to destroy the enemies of Earth.

He was dreaming of the traitor's last words to him, her last words to anyone, knowing she was about to die in the way she herself had killed an earlier fallen SEAL to complete her training. Would Killshot be sent to the arena as a traitor to the planet, one to be killed by or to kill a young candidate striving for completion of his or her own dream? The candidates didn't always win, far from it. But eventually the disgraced soldier would die at the hands of someone who knew only his own ambition, someone who would consider his opponent's label as a traitor "not his problem."

There was a moment when Killshot realized he was passing from dreaming into thinking about the dream, and that meant consciousness was imminent. He felt himself restrained against some kind of bed or other flat surface, and now he could comprehend he was hearing two men speaking in the room, probably the two apes that had scared off his mid-coitus comfort patriots and then beat the living hell out of him.

"It don't matter what she wants with him. She just wants him, and we got him," one of them said. "Hell, why does that woman do *anything*?"

The other snorted a laugh. "She seems to be doing okay. Wish I had her smarts—*I'd* be the one running this dump."

"You barely got the smarts to take your pants off before you take a shit."

Killshot didn't know if he should make some sort of sign that he was waking up. Would they start their abuse again on a man chained to a bed? They didn't seem especially refined. What were they, henchmen for some woman crime boss? *I'd be the one running this dump*, the one had said. Did that mean that this woman they were talking about *was* the one running things? And what did "running things" even mean? Was he still in the brothel, or near it, or even in any area of the resort planet he would remotely recognize?

Only one way to find out. He forced open his swollen and blood-crusted eyes and said weakly through fattened lips, "Fellas."

They both jumped like he had screamed into their ears. Immediately abashed, they shook it off as best they could to save face in front of their captive. "You're awake," the blond one said in a feat of observational skill.

"Not your fault," Killshot said.

"Huh?"

"He's a smart-mouth," the dark-haired thug said. "Miss Symantha won't take to that real good, will she?"

"No?" Blondie said.

47

Dark-hair let out a tired sigh.

Killshot wanted to laugh, but his bruised cheeks and throbbing head seemed to indicate that wasn't a good idea right then, especially since, he could see now, he was tied with metal cord to the four corners of a small bed that itself looked chained to the wall of the subterranean-feeling room. If this room was part of the brothel, it sure wasn't the fun part.

"So, gentlemen," he said, "may I assist you in some manner?"

"You're one of them SEALs the War Council is looking for," the dark-haired one said. "One of the Enhanced ones, right?"

Oh, no. The shit he found himself in seemed to be much deeper all of a sudden. "Um … *nuq vIghel SoH vISovbe'.*" Essentially, this was a combination of "No idea what you're talking about" by way of *"No comprendo, señor."*

"SoHvaD Qo'?" [Don't you?]

Great, I get the one knuckle-dragger in the galaxy who's also an alien linguist. "All right. But come on, guys, if I were on the run from the Council, they'd be here themselves to arrest me."

The blond one smiled with his big, square teeth. It was unsettling. "Only if they knew you was here."

Killshot swallowed.

"But the War Council *doesn't* know you're here. That a Space Navy platoon of traitors are running around on Altair, drinking, screwing, having the time of their lives."

"Oh yeah, what a party," Killshot said. "If you know how SEALs work, you know that they don't spill anything to anybody. Not even if you torture them."

"S'fun anyways," Blondie said. "I'm more, whaddya call it, *process-oriented.*"

"So you admit you're a SEAL," Dark said. "We're halfway there, then."

Goddamnit.

"Let's go the rest of the way. You from the crashed Navy ship, the one the Council put out the subspace reward call for? The *Blue Seltzer?*"

"*Celeste,*" Killshot said automatically, and shut his eyes in defeat. If that wasn't the oldest trick in the book, it was definitely on a nearby page.

"Miss Symantha's gonna be happy as a clamp," Blondie said. Dark and Killshot actually shared a roll of their eyes.

"Listen, you told us what we need to know, all right? We don't need to hurt you any worse."

"I'm a Space-Earth Aggression Leaper, man. You don't need to spare me jack shit."

"So … you *want* us to torture you?"

"I'd rather you didn't. I'm just saying I could take it. Space Navy SEAL right here is what I'm saying."

"More like *ex*-SEAL, from what the War Council is saying. Traitors and such."

"They betrayed us first," Killshot said. What point was there in dissembling now? "They were turning dedicated soldiers and sailors into monsters."

"Not our problem," Dark said, and Killshot recoiled as if he had been slapped. "What?"

"Nothing." He took as deep a breath as he could with his injuries. "So, you got me. Are you turning me over to the Council then, get the reward?"

"Nah, our job was just to get you down here. You and Miss Symantha are going to have a talk, and then she'll decide if she can use you or kill you."

Blondie giggled. "The Council's got a 'Dead or Alive' thing going on. You dumbass traitors are skuh-*rewed*."

I'm not a traitor.

Not my problem.

You're a traitor if the Powers That Be say you're a traitor. The only time you stop believing that is when they say *you're* a traitor. And then it's too goddamn late, isn't it?

Blond put a finger up to his ear, apparently listening to someone speaking into his feed. He said to Dark, "She's coming up. We should sit him up or something, right?"

Dark seemed to consider it, but said, "Nah, let him feel what it's like to be helpless in front of Miss Symantha." Then, to Killshot: "Seriously, the sooner you learn that, the better."

The metal door slid open. It wasn't automatic like the doors in the brothel or on the ship … or anywhere else Killshot had been in his twenty-seven years. No, this was *old* old school, like maybe pre-War old school, and the grating of the underground tunnel door against its track was terrifying, like things were out of control.

Yeah, *like* things were out of control. He almost smiled.

A woman who had to be "Miss Symantha" strode through the opened door, and some lackey on the other side pushed the heavy metal plate closed. She was flanked by two men, a skinny one who looked like a stage magician gone to seed with his thin moustache and battered (*tuxedo? Is that what those are called?*) black suit; and a jackrabbit-nervous even-skinnier one dressed in ...

... a goddamn Space Navy leapsuit. It was dirty as hell and patched sloppily here and there, but that had definitely belonged to a SEAL. Killshot kept his Enhanced eyes on him and read the faded nametag: OPPERMAN.

That wasn't the name of anybody he knew, but platoons didn't mix much—except on places like Altair—so this shaking bag of bones could be a disgraced SEAL long in hiding for all Killshot knew. If these were her bodyguards instead of Blondie and Dark, Miss Symantha might want to rethink her personnel choices.

The woman was of an impossible-to-discern age: she might have been thirty, she might have been fifty. However old she was, the red satin dress she wore hugged her hips and everything else on her body in a way that would have made Killshot's mouth water if he hadn't just had his salivary glands put through a tad bit of abuse. As it was, he licked his lips to wet them, not lasciviously but because he knew he would be expected to talk to this raven-haired, ice-cold ... whatever she was.

"You are [Killshot's real name] from the crashed ship in Flynt Plateau." Not a question.

So he gave no answer.

Her hot-rod-red lips turned up in a smirk. "No bullshit. I like that. So, Mister Killshot, I'm sure Chalk and Cheese over here told you who I am." The thugs nodded for him. "Can you guess *what* I am? What I'm doing down here with a traitor Space Navy Aggression Specialist?"

That was a Space *Army* designation, but he sure as hell wasn't going to correct her. His eyes went to the twitchy dude in the leapsuit. He licked his lips again, cleared his throat, and carefully pronounced through his cracked and swollen mouth, "I don't know your line, lady, but you're the boss or outer space ain't cold."

She bent back and let out a hearty but unmistakably feminine laugh. "Oh, I think I'm going to like you, Killshot," she said, and stepped up to the bed he was bound to, her bookends staying back. "So, clever man, do you want to know what it is I'm the boss *of* here on Resort Central?"

Play it safe, he told himself. "I'm mildly curious."

She chuckled—again, in the way one would expect a vidstar to, silky and inviting—and said, "I run … *things* … on Altair."

"Things. Safe to assume we don't mean a chain of laundromats?"

"Safe, indeed, Mister Killshot. I have my fingers in almost every pie on the planet: highly illegal weaponry, highly coveted psychoactive substances of all kinds, highly profitable but illegal casinos, highly coveted prostitutes—and I'm not talking about those sad-sack 'comfort patriots.' I'm talking about sexual acrobats who can make you feel anything they want to. Anything *you* want to."

"I wouldn't mind having my finger in that pie."

"Ha! I'm the highly organized bad mama of this planet's highly organized crime. You know all these things operate on Altair, I assume. You don't look *especially* naïve."

"Thanks?"

Just a smile this time. Maybe his cute act was wearing thin. If so, that was unfortunate, because that was pretty much the only arrow he had in his quiver right now. "As the boss of this particular planet of fun, I'm quite interested in money, as many credits as I can squeeze out of you soldiers and sailors. But there's one thing I want more, although it will lead to much more income for your hostess."

"I am now going to ask what that thing is," he said. "Say, Miss Symantha, what might that *highly desirable* thing be?"

She sat on the edge of the bed and leaned in close to his face, and *goddamn*, she smelled even better than she looked, an achievement in itself. "There is one racket on Altair that I can't seem to crack. I've offered riches, I've offered access to my own personal sex, I've threatened violence, and I've had that violence carried out time and time again."

Shit, Killshot thought, *what the hell could this be?*

"There's an … well, let's call it an *operation* on the other side of the planet, far from Sin Disney, one that is so profitable that I would wield influence far beyond Altair, far beyond this entire *system*."

He waited. "So … you gonna tell me what this no-doubt-unsavory enterprise might be?"

She sat back up, but remained seated on the bed. "Not yet. How do I know if I can trust you?"

Now he laughed, despite himself. "*Trust*? I would say at the moment, tied to this dirty-ass bed like a hillbilly sacrifice, that no, you can't trust me."

She smiled again, her lips parting over perfectly white teeth this time. "What if I told you that the War Council is offering a reward for information leading to your arrest and execution, or, if you meet with some misfortune, for your head and ID chip in a bag?"

"I'm gonna get crazy and say that you *are* telling me that."

"Just so, Mister Killshot. May I call you 'Killshot'?"

"What are titles between old friends like us, Symantha?"

Her eye twitched, so slightly and quickly that without his special vision he would have missed it entirely. "Agreed." She stood and smoothed her Saturn-satin dress. "You could buy a mine on Vesta with the amount the Council is offering for *any* of the heads of you traitors. If somebody collected all of you enemies in the Council's War, she could probably *buy* Vesta."

"That does sound remunerative." The more he talked, the less his lips and cheeks hurt. It made getting threatened with death and such almost worth the bother. "If I see any of those fellows, I'll be sure to send them your way."

She laughed again and said to Dark and Blond, "Cut him loose. He'll behave."

"I will mind my manners like no one's ever minded theirs before."

The big men cut through the cords—*oh, holy hell*, the blood returning to his hands and feet was more painful than anything the thugs had doled out—and sat Killshot up on the bed. Gently, even. They must have been scared out of their wits at this luscious dragon lady.

He didn't blame them.

"I have a choice, then. Should I turn you over to the Council— they have spies here, of course, and I'm sure they know you at least *were* on-world—or should I enlist you for my little project? It would take you to the far side of the planet, someplace those shits *never* go."

Killshot blinked. He had no idea such a place existed in this part of the galaxy. "That's not much of a choice. The Council isn't my favorite group of people right now."

"Not *much* of a choice? My dear, it's not a choice for you to make at all. I said *I* have a choice."

"How can I help?" he said with a blood-crusted smile.

She turned and indicated the pencil-necked magician. "Before you tell me what you can do for me, I'd like to introduce two of the foot soldiers I've already enlisted. This young man is Presto— not his real name, of course."

"You don't say."

"Presto is what you would call an 'Enhanced' soldier in the Space Army, or at least that's what he was before he went AWOL on Altair and became a stage prestidigitator."

Killshot found himself staring at the once-well-dressed man, and had to shake himself out of it. "Dude," he said, "why the hell would you do that? You had to know they'd come after you."

Presto sought approval from his boss before saying to Killshot, "The Council ordered us to occupy a Xeno settlement in the Xylcher system, letting none of them in or out. We were ordered to take what the sentients considered food and leave them to starve. I didn't question anything—I was an Enhanced λ-560 Beret, and they don't just hand out that designation—but it was *months*. The Xenos had language and building knowledge, but no weapons beyond bronze swords and shields.

"That doesn't matter, I know that—they *could* do it in the future, and then be capable of destroying the rest of Earth—"

You mean Terra? was Killshot's automatic thought, so used to making fun with the platoon about the Space Army. *Dang donkey-*

ass foot soldiers. He suppressed what would have been a callously timed smile.

"—but why *starve* them? Why make their young wail in that species's nerve-rattling way, for goddamn *months*? We Berets didn't have any assignment other than blockading this one settlement. Hell, SEALs and Space Army units wiped out the rest of the life on the planet—why were we torturing the poor alien bastards? I'd been through a couple of tours and killed who knows how many bugs and sentients, but I'd never even *heard* of the Council ordering this. On top of everything else, what a waste of resources!"

"I never heard of that, either," Killshot said, sickened. *Weakened* inside, somehow. "Shit, man."

"Eventually they all died, of course. Our assignment was done, so we left. I didn't find out until we were having R & R here on Altair that the Council had vidded the entire thing, running the footage every night on Earth vidscreens, displaying to all mankind that we were showing the enemy no mercy. *No* mercy, not even what you'd show an insect on our planet. They had the 'show' on the vidscreens all over the resorts, and people even recognized me—*they shook my goddamn hand.* When my platoon headed off Altair for our next assignment, I stayed behind. They looked for me, thinking something bad had happened, but couldn't find me and couldn't find anybody who knew anything. That's because no one *did* know. I took my rations and dug myself a pit in the surface, staying there for a week, monitoring communications until I knew they had given me up for dead. Then I got ahold of some fancy clothes, changed my appearance, and started doing magic to blend in."

"*To blend in?*"

"Yeah, hiding in plain sight, all of that. My—my *Enhancement*—allows me to cloud the minds of any human or even Xeno looking directly at me. Not a lot, but enough to make sentients miss me with their weapons and even the biggest bugs lose me entirely. Watch." The magician looked directly at Killshot, who was of course concentrating on him—and disappeared. Not swishing a cape or going up in a puff of smoke: Presto was just there one moment and gone the next.

Killshot gave his head a shake and blinked. No, the Beret had vanished.

A finger tapped him on the shoulder. It was Presto, now behind him. He did it again, and there he was, right where he had been initially.

Killshot laughed in amazement. "That's one hell of an Enhancement."

"Yeah, well, it worked great until about a year later, when my old unit came back to Altair for their resort break and one of my old mates saw me. She knew exactly who I was—and went to notify her commander and the nearest Council operative that she had found a deserter, a traitor in the War. I didn't consider refusing to do anything so dishonorable again to be treasonous, but my old mate sure as hell did. And the Council definitely would have. You know that, you're a SEAL, or were. Wipe your ass wrong and they label you a traitor."

I'm not a traitor.

Not my problem.

He closed his eyes in shame, the first feeling of real *shame* since he had passed the test to join the elite Space Navy squads. He couldn't really even imagine the shame that this Lambda must have experienced in order to desert the Space Army. But then he realized what Presto had said and opened his eyes in confusion. "Wait … they *would have?*"

"Damned straight, Killshot," Miss Symantha said with a real smile. "I knew who this fallen Lambda was and what he could do. I went to see his show, and *nobody* is *that* good at legerdemain. I did a little nosing around and learned who he was. When he was discovered—and it had to happen eventually, since Council spies pay handsomely for information—I swooped in and rescued him from being hung by his balls in public, with Council vidcams capturing every screaming second."

Presto all of a sudden looked down at his tattered shoes.

Symantha noticed and gave a very genuine chuckle at her employee's obvious discomfort. She turned from him to Killshot and said, "I *might* have been the one to tip off his former platoon-mate. But I wanted him, and that was the way to bring him right into my arms. And I *did* save his life, regardless of how he was discovered, right?"

"Yes, Miss Symantha," he mumbled like he had a gun to his head. "Thank you."

"That's really interesting," Killshot said. "So should I assume you go around rescuing stray military men and making them wear the same clothes for years on end while they serve you in some capacity?"

She laughed in that way that requires only the exhalation of breath through the nose and a sour, insincere movement of the mouth that could indicate either distaste or ... well, no, just distaste. "I'm not in the charity business—actually, I am, but that orphanage is a credit-laundering front, and anyway, this largesse doesn't extend to my rescue animals." She reconsidered and added, "Or it doesn't until we make this new enterprise a success. Then you guys get your freedom, a new identity, and more credits than you'll know how to spend."

"Wait, 'you guys'? I don't remember signing up for anything."

"Opperman, tell Johnny Independent here why he's already signed on the dotted line."

So his name really is *Opperman. That means those tattered rags were once his SEAL leapsuit.* This was not a happy revelation, especially considering the tremors and shakes striking every part of Opperman's body from his eyelids to his knees.

The shaking, emaciated-looking former SEAL placed his gaze on Killshot for really the first time since Symantha's entourage had entered the bunker. "I said no to M-M-Miss Syman-n-n-tha's offer," he said, his stutter seeming just another part of his unceasing trembling. "Sh-she turned m-m-me in."

"To whom did I turn you in, Opperman?"

He squeezed his eyes shut like a child watching a horror vidshow. "It. It. It ... *It* ... i-i-it ..."

Symantha rolled her eyes and said to the poor son of a bitch, "Pull it together, soldier."

"It w ... w-was ..."

"You turned him in to the goddamn War Council?" Killshot said sharply, but far less sharply than he felt like saying.

"Indeed I did, got the reward and everything," she said. "When the giant meat slabs over there went in to pull him out—some hands had to be greased, I admit, or it would have been impossible—our former Lieutenant Opperman was … *this*."

Opperman had shut his eyes again.

"He was there, what, three days?" she said to Dark-hair, who nodded. "They tortured him so thoroughly in just seventy-two hours that … well, you can see for yourself."

Killshot wished he could stand up and kill this bitch with his bare hands, but there was too much muscle and too many Enhanced drones in the room to do any such thing. "What's he got that's so valuable?"

"He's Enhanced, like you. Unfortunately for him, he used that Enhancement to stop his commander from shooting his platoon-mate execution-style in the head for refusing a direct order."

Killshot didn't know where to start with this, and he could feel his throat constricting again. But he chose: "What was the order?"

In addition to the horrid shaking of his body, Opperman now shook his head back and forth, as if saying *no* to reliving what had happened.

Symantha said, "Do you know what 'Russian Roulette' is?"

Killshot nodded. It couldn't be "played" with particle beam sidearms, of course, but replicas of the centuries-old revolver pistols weren't hard to find. Russia didn't even exist anymore—almost no nation-states did after the Alien Aggression—but everybody knew what Russian Roulette was. "You use those old pistols, the ones where you had to put the bullets in the revolving chamber. You take out five of the bullets, leaving just one, and then you spin the chamber. Then you put the gun to your head and pull the trigger. You got a one-in-six chance of blowing your brains out."

"All right, Lieutenant History! Now, do you know what Polish Roulette is?"

Polish Roulette? He remembered vaguely that there had been a country called Poland. Was it part of Russia? Why would there be *Polish* Roulette? "No, ma'am, I don't."

Her face cracked into a wicked smile. "You *remove* only one bullet."

"You're shitting me. Was that commander insane? Why would he make Opperman play—"

"No, it wasn't our shuddering friend here. It was his mate in the platoon, someone who had committed some minor violation of protocol. I don't know, didn't have his boots tied right, whatever, and remember this was on Altair, where you assholes are *supposed* to cut loose. So yes, indeed, their boss was completely insane. He put the pistol in that soldier's hand and told him it was time to see if God wanted to grant him clemency."

This is a nightmare, Killshot thought with desperation. *I'm still unconscious. Maybe I'm dead.*

But he was wide awake, and he knew it.

"Opperman, you want to tell our new friend what happened next?"

"Oh, shit—did that guy point the gun on the chief? Did he shoot the son of a bitch?"

The trembling ex-SEAL shook his head. "H-he poured the b-b-bullets on the g-ground."

This time Killshot closed *his* eyes. *Jumping Jovian Jesus. Cosmic Crapping Christ.*

"That was all it took. Their commander forced him to kneel in front of him and called him—"

I'm not

"—a traitor and was about to send a full metal jacket right into his brain. Opperman here saw what was about to happen and knew the insanity behind it and jumped in to save his friend."

Not my problem.

Killshot felt more weary now than after any battle he'd ever been through. "You used your Enhancement?" At Opperman's nod, he asked, not even wanting to know the answer, "What is it?"

"M-m-move," he said, indicating the bed. Killshot stood a bit painfully and moved out of the space between Opperman and what he could now think of only as "the torture bed."

Opperman took a deep, deep breath, held it for a moment, and then exhaled through his mouth a hail of projectiles that turned the dirty mattress into a cloud of pale foam bits and reduced the metal frame to a barely recognizable pile of shards. Then the former

SEAL, shaking noticeably less for the moment, looked at Killshot and gave him the slightest of nods. "K-k-killed him good," he said.

"You're a human railgun," Killshot said in amazement. "You breathe in the air's water vapor and extract the hydrogen and oxygen to make hydronium …"

"And freeze them into bullets, yes," Symantha finished for him. "He can exhale them at deadly speed, too—not at the velocity of a real railgun, but plenty fast."

Killshot could feel that his mouth was open. He collected himself and said, "I had no idea they could do that with Enhancement technology."

"Oh, the War Council is moving ahead with all sorts of aggressive new initiatives. But I guess you know that, don't you? You were supposed to be part of one yourself, but you and your platoon got a bit *uppity*." She *tsk-tsk*ed ironically. "The Council would *love* to get their mitts on you, my traitorous friend. They'd make what they did to poor Opperman here look like a bubble bath."

For a moment, no one spoke. Symantha and Killshot stared at each other, and everybody else stared at them staring at each other.

"Before you ask, *yes*. I will turn you over to the Council spies to do what they will with you. I want you and your vision Enhancement to help me grow my operation, and what I want, I get. Isn't that right, gentlemen?"

They all practically tripped over their own tongues to voice their absolute agreement.

"So, do we have an agreement? Wouldn't you rather have the carrot than the stick? Opperman got the stick, and once he knew he'd be going back if he didn't please me, he chose the carrot."

Opperman still shook, but his nod was perceptible.

"Why don't you save yourself a *lot* of trouble and just help me get my carrot, huh?"

"All right," Killshot said at last, and was a little embarrassed at how relieved he was to hear himself assent. "I'm in. But I need one concession from you, Symantha."

"I think we'll go back to *Miss* Symantha, if you please."

"I need one thing. You know everything that goes on in the brothels, the bars, the gambling halls, all of that, right?"

"Killshot, I *own* 'all of that.'"

"Great. Then I need to know where my buddy is. He has a hearing Enhancement that can really help you ... but he could be in bed with any comfort patriot, thrown out into a gutter, arrested by the Council, anything. You help me find him, he'll join us, I guarantee it."

"That's it? Find your whoring platoon-mate? Consider it done, Killshot. I know exactly where he is."

Whew. "Thank you, Symantha."

Her eyes narrowed. "Don't get cocky. I can have you in a Council torture chamber before you can even shit yourself with fear."

"All right, *Miss* Symantha. Roger that."

***

Inman hadn't made a single sound since that last powerful bolt of electricity through his thorax. He fell asleep—more like passed out—despite the bulky collar, but woke up when it popped open along with the ones binding his wrists and ankles. He shook himself fully awake and said in a raspy voice, "What, is that it? I can go?"

"Not so fast, ho-boy," a smug voice came, originating in the fat man who came into focus in front of Inman. "Time to start paying society back for your crimes, shitpile."

"Is this a joke? I'm a goddamn Space Navy SEAL! What is going on?"

The fat man grabbed Inman by the throat and stood him up by squeezing it. His foul face came forward until Inman wanted to gag from his breath as much as being choked. "You mean a goddamn *former* Space Navy SEAL, dontcha? You think word don't get around? You're a comfort patriot now, *traitor*—and you sitting around all day in shiny underpants is a hell of a lot nicer than what you'd get if I turned your ass in to the authorities."

Inman had nothing to say to that, so he said nothing.

"Speaking of your ass, you got your first customer, Jack. Welcome to our humble establishment," Fatty said, turning Inman around and shoving him forward. "Room 42—I believe you know just where that is."

Don't panic, he repeated to calm himself. *Don't panic. You love sex, women, and even the occasional man if the mood is right. Just don't panic and run or do something else stupid and end up incurably dead.*

"Just do your job for the next coupla cycles and you can retire," Fatty said, then fat-man chortled before adding, "I hear Ceres is lovely this time of year."

He pushed Inman again, and the ex-SEAL started shuffling toward Room 42—which was one he once used for his R & R fun with CPs, nice and ironic—because he didn't know what else to do. Could sex, even if it wasn't on his schedule, be that bad? (Probably, after 24/7 shifts for a couple of years.) He knew the brothel didn't allow grievous bodily harm to be done to their "workers" and knew it from the experience of an unwell former platoon-mate getting barred entirely and indefinitely from the entire resort planet network. Inman didn't know what ever happened to that mate, but he never heard from him again. He wondered if the poor sap had gone Section 8 nuts because there was no chance for rest between massacres, ever.

Inman got to the door and took a deep breath. He was poised to knock when the door slid open and a *very* attractive woman—not Fugly-glamour attractive, but still heart-achingly hot—stood there smiling, wearing a knee-length black negligée, and welcomed him into the room. "We requested you specifically," she said, her smile infectious. "My name is Peggy. You're the new meat, right?"

New meat didn't sound like something he particularly wanted to be, but he nodded and allowed her to take his hand and guide him into the spacious suite, which was much nicer than the usual bang-spots a soldier could afford. (He had hit a jackpot in the resort casino once and rented this room to "entertain" a series of sex slaves one crazy night.)

"Ladies?" she called out, and sure enough, three other *very* attractive women—could they be actual military, or just off-world hotties looking for fun?—stepped out from each doorway in the suite, clad just like the supermodel who had greeted him at the door. "I'd like you to meet our new friend, Mister ... ?" She prompted him with a dazzling smile.

Don't say your real name, Inman reminded himself. "Underhill."

"How nice. Well, off with those space shorts, Mister Underhill, and let's get down to business."

Inman stammered as the ladies sat on the plush U-shaped sofa in the sunken center of the main room, "I'm, uh, not really hard, you know, kinda nervous, um ..."

"That's not a problem. Drop your pants, *now*."

He did as she told him, and the ladies gazed in appreciation at his "short-arm," which, even not fully tumescent, was a sight to behold. They giggled a little and looked to their leader.

"While you prepare yourself, let me introduce my friends. We aren't military, but we are looking for a *good* time, you understand?"

He said jovially, "Hey, you don't have to be a soldier to want—"

"Speak when I tell you to speak, *slave*."

The word made him quiver with panic. He almost said "Okay," but that was speaking, and she hadn't told him to speak. He got the feeling that he'd stay clamped in the shock collar in the lobby for a long time if he annoyed these first customers.

"Good." She waved a hand at the fiery redhead in a white nightie. "This is Peggy."

Peggy? Wasn't the hostess's name Peggy? But he didn't say a damned thing.

Peggy #2 gave a coy wave of her fingers. She may have been even hotter than Peggy #1.

He was then introduced to Peggys #3 and #4. They all looked excited, and he bet he just looked confused as shit, because he was. What was with all the Peggys? That was an unusual name in the first place.

Just play along, follow their lead. This is sex, paid sex, and you know how this works better than anybody, he told himself. *Just play along with everybody, Fatty included, until you can get the hell out of here.*

"You're all named Peggy? That's … interesting." At least he wouldn't call anyone by the wrong name.

Peggy #1, the hostess, put her fingers around his growing member and, by that, led him to the couch, where she had them both sit down. "Slave, our names aren't really Peggy. That's more of a nickname, really."

"Oh, yeah? You all have the same nickname, then. Also interesting. How did that happen?"

The girls all looked at each other and barely suppressed their laughter. One by one, each stood up to face where Inman was seated right at the bottom of the U-shaped couch. Then each lifted the front of her knee-length negligée.

Strapped to each beautiful woman was a sizeable dildo, each one bigger than the last. "Slave, have you ever heard of 'pegging'? Because that's why we're all called Peggy."

Inman knew what pegging was. Oh god, he knew. His mind told him again not to panic, but he went ahead and panicked. He stayed very still and didn't make a peep, but his body felt like it was going into shock. He'd been with a man or two in his sexual career, but that was mostly kissing and sucking with a little bit of backdoor stuff, and his backdoor had never accommodated anything two-thirds the size of the ginormous cudgels attached around the slim waists of these women.

"You get it now?" Peggy #1 asked with a big ol' smile. She lined them up single-file in front of Inman, the smallest—but still pornvid-sized—dong in front and then moving up in size to the tremendous proportions of Peggy #1's at the end.

Peggy #4, a girl with the face of an angel and the artificial penis of a demon from Hell, guided him to turn around as she said in her sweet voice, "Ass forward, honey." Peggy #1 cleared her throat loudly, and Peggy #4 corrected herself: "I mean, *slave.*"

This cannot be happening. But it was, of course, so he said the only thing that could come to his mind, which was, "Do you ladies use Hyperion lube? It's the best on the m—"

"No, butt-slave. It doesn't matter to us if it's rough or smooth. These aren't nerve-connected dildonics, just plain monsters for fun," Peggy #1 said lightly. "Peggy"—she was calling Peggy #4— let's get this party started!"

Peggy #4 did just that, and after a few minutes Inman realized his screaming only made the ladies more aroused and peg him harder.

***

It could have been an hour or could have been a week later as far as Inman could tell—trauma, blood, passing out, *being revived*, trauma, blood, passing out—the cycle had wrecked more than his ass. As Fatty held him up and brought him back to his place in the seat against the wall (but which now had towels laid on it), Inman felt like he had lost his mind as well.

Fatty gingerly set him down on the three inches of soft towels. "The first day is a rough one," he said in what sounded almost like a sympathetic tone, "but don't you worry, traitor—there's just ten and a half hours left in your shift." He patted Inman on the shoulder, maybe. He waddled away, Inman was confident he saw that. And the neck and other clamps closed back around him, that *definitely* happened. He hoped his weeping wouldn't set off the shock collar.

In a few minutes, counting the throbs carried Inman into exhausted sleep. He had a dream, no doubt caused by the pain he could feel even through the veil of unconsciousness, that his next customer made the Peggys seem like they had given him a backrub. And the next was worse. And the next, and the next, stretching out—even his sleeping brain cringed at the words— indefinitely into the future.

Out of all of the other "comfort patriots" being punished for crimes against the state like loose talk, missing the weekly provincial head count because of a sick child, or maybe refusing to fulfill their compulsory military stint in the War on Alien Aggression, Inman realized he may have been the one most guilty of actual treason. Blowing up an entire Council research planet was no minor break in protocol—and even *he* didn't deserve this. How many CPs had he enjoyed without ever giving the slightest crap about their situation? If his head hadn't already been bent at an angle from passing out inside the collar, he would have hung it in shame.

The *click-tap-click-tap-click-tap* of stiletto heels getting louder and then stopping just in front of him compelled Inman to open his eyes and take in the exotic woman dressed like the emperor's favorite concubine, long black hair swept over her shoulders. "Mister Inman?"

"Oh, god, not yet."

She laughed and put her hands into a single clap of amusement. "How do you like life in my brothel? Comfort patriots are the best free labor a girl ever had, let me tell you. Thank you for your service," she said, surely an intentionally ironic take on what grateful Terran citizens universally said to their military protectors.

"You *own* this place?" Inman asked in real surprise, then looked around again at his defeated compatriots in despair. "Aren't you *ashamed* of yourself?"

Symantha's smile twitched slightly. "There would be nothing *to* own if it weren't for the loyal business of horny soldiers and sailors like you. And not just *like* you—I mean *you*, too."

"Believe me, I have seen the light."

"And your buddy, what's his name?"

Inman's blood froze. He didn't want to say a goddamn thing to this woman, it went against all his training, but he was the one here bolted to a chair with a high chance of receiving (more) internal injuries, so he decided to skip any resistance to this she-devil who obviously held every card there was to hold. "I take it you mean Lieutenant [real name]? Killshot?"

"Well, it would be a bit disingenuous to call him anything but '*ex*-lieutenant,' *n'est-ce pas*? No sense in denying the shit soup you and your fellow traitors from the *Blue Celeste* have found yourself in."

Despite the pain, Inman's joy made him straighten from his slouch. "You've found them? They're alive?"

"Down, boy," the woman said, and waved over the fat keeper of the CPs. "We've found this 'Killshot,' and he's joined our little operation. We thought that you might be interested in helping out as well."

Inman waited for her to go on, but then went ahead and said, "What's the operation?"

"It's none of your goddamn business, ass-boy. Join us or we'll just leave you here to rot with the rest of the traitors. That is, if you aren't already dying of internal bleeding."

Inman's face said everything Miss Symantha needed to know. "The Peggys are a tough group of bitches, aren't they? You wouldn't be the first CP whose career they cut extremely short."

"Wait—you know who chose me?"

She motioned for Fatty to undo the clamps and help Inman up. The towels were soaked through with blood, as were his shiny shorts, from which rivulets of gore trickled. "Of course I know—who do you think got you all together? I told you, I own this modest den of iniquity, and I want to expand my horizons. I thought a visit from the Peggys might make you more ... *amenable* ... to getting on the team."

Had she *set him up*? "You did this to me, and you expect that to make me *want to help you*?"

She laughed again and said, "You should be *begging* to help me, Mister Inman. Otherwise, I'm going to leave you right where you are. If you don't die, you'll soon wish you had. But if you do come on board, we'll get your damage all fixed up, you'll get to see your buddy Killshot again, and if we succeed in seizing the final piece of my becoming overlord of Altair, you'll be richer than the Potentate of Pluto, the Czar of diamond Cancri—"

"More real liquidity than Roderick LaRoux?"

"Ha! Sorry, that one's reserved for me," she said, and Inman got the feeling she liked their gentle sparring. "But you and your mate could be so wealthy the War Council would just tell the world you were killed for your treachery and then forget you ever existed."

Inman managed a smile, though it was tempered by his pain. "But what if we can't seize ... whatever it is you want to seize?"

She put her hand on his arm, and although he would have expected it to feel as cold as her eyes looked, it was warm and smooth and inviting. "Don't worry, my dear. If you desert my operation, my men will find you in hours and you'll be right back here, forever. But you wouldn't do that to me, would you?"

"I am gonna go ahead and say no."

"Good boy." She now motioned to Fatty to get his lackeys to bring a stretcher, and they gently lifted Inman onto it, face down, his ruined ass on display for anyone with the stomach to look at it. "But stay with the gang. If we succeed, life will be happy for all of us. If we fail, you'll all be dead and won't have to worry about anything ever again."

"Wait—*we'll* all be dead? Aren't you part of the operation?"

"You and the boys will do just fine. You're all Enhanced and love to kill. Besides, my clothes are too nice to get dirty. Even more than that, this planet depends on me running its multifarious and profitable side businesses. I can't die. I'm *Miss Symantha*, Mister Inman."

Being wheeled away, Inman said, "You got yourself a deal, you sadistic goddamn bitch. I say that in admiration. You're like the love child of Nick Machiavelli and Vlad Harkonnen, and that's just me being nice."

Symantha laughed hard and waved goodbye to Inman as he was rolled back to the brothel's emergency medical area, usually reserved for damage inflicted by johns but also with a staff used to rebuilding vaginas, recreating rectums, and rescuing male genitalia. Unlike his smart-mouth brother-in-arms, this Inman was someone she could see herself not hating.

She had a crew with all the Enhancements needed to seize or— if she couldn't take it by force—burn that goddamn Council farm on the other side of Altair right to the ground. They would leave the next day at sunset and get over there by the time night was falling—and darkness was the schemer's friend. She now had Killshot's Enhanced vision, Inman's Enhanced hearing, Opperman's human railgun Enhancement, and Presto's Enhanced ability to confuse and dismay any enemy. Now all she needed for victory was some real muscle armed with the very weapons she sold to both sides of the War on Alien Aggression.

Her dream was to collect the rest of the Enhanced survivors of the *Blue Celeste* and get them all working for her to seize her prize, but she hadn't received word yet of any other sightings by her man on the ground. Still, she had reason to believe the traitorous crew would all be herded to the Council farm by the time Altair's sun came up there. They wouldn't be working for her, exactly, it was true, but they could all work toward the same goal, even if it were for completely unrelated reasons. The traitors had no cause to love the War Council anymore.

But there was still a lot of work to be done to make that happen. It would be morning before everything was ready, but she was lying when she said she wouldn't be there. *Of course* she would see her empire on Altair take its huge bite to consume the final bit she didn't already control. So she would rest, and god help the assholes who worked for her if they couldn't depart at first light.

With a renewed smile, Miss Symantha started back for her chambers, *click-tap-click-tap-click-tap*.

3

When Gunner awoke from the crash, he found himself hanging by his chute straps from one of the bulbous-limbed native Altair trees. They weren't really trees in the sense of Terran trees—they were more like extremely slow-moving animals that did photosynthesize sugars from the system's sun but which also could use their appendages to signal one another. No sensory organs had been discovered on the tree-things, but they seemed able both to see and hear signals made by others of their species. Luckily, Gunner surmised two minutes after he came back to consciousness, his tree was mellow and in no apparent hurry to go anywhere, even for an Altairian tree.

However, something less lucky stood in front of the tree, something that held what Gunner could tell (being a gunnery sergeant, after all) was a high-voltage rifle that could be set to tase a target into painful submission or burn it to death from the inside out. The weapon-carrier was clad entirely in brown, his or her head shrouded within a hood, dark goggles hiding what might have been visible of the person's eyes. It was an intimidating sight, but when you've just fallen thousands and thousands of feet to the surface after being spun off an uncontrollably spiraling spacecraft, your tank for intimidation was pretty full.

"Help you, stranger?" Gunner said as sunnily as he could. "I like your rifle there—what is that, a tri-barrel Jackhammer?"

The dark stranger smiled with strangely gleaming teeth and aimed his weapon at the chute straps holding Gunner to the tree. He fired, and the plasma arced through the air to eat through one strap, then another blast took out the other one. Gunner fell only about ten feet, but they were a long ten with nothing but scrabble and dirt and rocks to break his fall.

"Thanks," he said, rubbing his hip as he stood, "I think."

The figure nodded and said in a slimy-feeling male voice, "You're from the *Blue Celeste*."

"What's that? A whorehouse around here? Maybe a gambling hall?"

"I'm a collector for the War Council, gunnery sergeant. Or can I call you 'Gunner'?"

"Call me whatever you want, man. I'm just a tourist."

The stranger leveled the Jackhammer at him. "A tourist wearing a Space Navy standard-issue SEAL jumpsuit. One that says 'Blue Celeste' on its arm patches. One who was just hanging from a tree by his military-issue parachute. So, are you going to talk honestly with me, or how would you like me to run three thousand degrees of hot plasma right through your chest?"

"I must say I would not like that at all. I've used that weapon. Prefer being on *your* side of it, all things considered."

The man in the robes kept the Jackhammer trained on Gunner and said, "Do you know what War Council collectors do?"

"You're basically bounty hunters, right? No offense, it's an honest job and all that."

"We bring in traitors on the run," he said. "People like you."

"Is the Council expecting a lot of traitors to show up on a resort planet for some reason?"

"Altair has a little bit of everything, Mister Gunner. Everybody ends up here at some point. Or if not Altair, then some other resort planet where they can live out the remainder of their short lives screwing, drinking, gambling, and doing whatever else they can to blend in like the hedonists they are."

"So, this is it for me? You taking me in to the Council office here? See me strung up and all that?"

"This might surprise you," the man said, "but no. I have secured papers of clemency for you right in my pocket, backed up with all the legal flexibility the War Council grants its collection specialists."

"All right. You've got my attention, friend."

"Bringing in one traitor from a platoon of Enhanced Space Navy SEALs pays good money, but presenting them all at once, chained in a line like animals to the Council office? I'll never have to work again. *You'll* never have to work again."

"Yeah, I'd never have to work again because I'd be *dead*," Gunner said, and gallows-laughed a little at his own words, but it was obvious that the man in the hood was serious. It was not lost on the gunnery sergeant that the stranger had lowered his weapon, no longer pointing it at him.

"I want to take you on as a partner, pardoned by the Council and eligible to receive a large sum for rounding up your fellow trai—that is, your former platoon."

As serious as the man may have seemed, Gunner had to ask, "I'm caught. I understand that and accept it. But what makes you think I would turn in my mates? I couldn't be happier if they got away, got the hell off this planet and were never, ever found by the goddamn War Council."

The stranger removed his dark goggles, but with his hood still on, all Gunner could make out were the unnatural glint of his eyes and his weirdly shiny teeth. He didn't seem especially psychotic or anything, but there was certainly something *off* about the man. "Did *you* make the decision to blow up L-22233?" the man asked. "Did *you* set off the Super-Nuke that killed everything on that planet, including the patriotic scientists and all those dedicated SEALs? I ask that because that's the way the Council is portraying it in their extensive propaganda throughout the human settlements in our part of the galactic arm: Every member of the crew of the *Blue Celeste* turned their backs on Earth and on the War Council that has kept humanity safe all these many years.

"So I ask you: Who took the mutinous, traitorous step of exploding that weapon of last resort, something made to be a deterrent, not to be exploded and its effects left like an open book to be examined by Xenos bent on Terran destruction?"

Gunner blinked. *Did he just say 'Terran'?* That was a SEAL term, used just between themselves. Shaking it off, he said, "I don't know exactly who made the decision to set it off. Maybe I agreed to it—in fact, I probably did. All of us *were* in on it, I'm sure."

"You have been taken for a ride, Gunner. Your commander and possibly your platoon-mates set you up to take the fall, at least partially."

"What? No, that's not possible—we're a tight-knit group—it's all of us or none of us—"

The stranger interrupted: "Look, that's nice and all, but I can help you keep your own personal testicles off the War Council chopping block. It doesn't matter to me—or the Council, to be honest—if one particular SEAL helped or didn't help. All I can tell you is that I possess the power to arrange amnesty and survival to *one* alleged traitor. I would like for that one person to be you."

"And what would this very special alleged traitor need to do for such agreeable treatment?"

He laughed with surprise. "Help me round up your fellows, of course! We'll present them together, they'll go to who knows what ignominious end, and you'll be free, completely pardoned by the Council."

"You underestimate the loyalty of a Space Navy SEAL."

"Loyal is as loyal does, my friend. I doubt I underestimate anyone's loyalty … to himself, that is. I definitely call into question the loyalty of every single SEAL who survived the crash of the *Blue Celeste*. Whomever I found first, I would make this same offer to that soldier. You were the first in this case, and you're lucky I could triangulate where you fell to ground—or to tree, in your case—before some other operative got to you. One not as personally, shall we say, *ambitious* as yours truly."

"So you'd have me be a double agent, traitor to the Council and then again to my mates."

"Psh, nonsense. You'd be a hero, not a traitor. A *rich* hero, at that, since I would share with you a sizeable portion of the bounty that the collection of all the other survivors as a group would bring." The stranger stopped talking for a moment and waited for Gunner to say something. When that didn't happen, he spoke again: "I need an answer now, if you please. Will you take on this very generous assignment?"

Gunner felt a tightness in his chest as he said, "How do we find my platoon-mates?"

"*We*? Is there a household deer in your pocket? This is a *you* situation, my new friend."

Should've figured, he thought, but said, "All right, how do *I* find them? And when I do, how do I get them to you?"

"I have good leads on where most all of them might be right now." The man reached into his wrap and pulled out a small black box with a grid-like readout on top. "This will lead you to find your fellows in arms. Just keep going until you get to where this leads you. Then you can coax whatever other ex-SEALs into the Council's waiting arms."

"How do I know they won't arrest *me*?"

"Gunner, yours is not the first ship of fools to try to escape the wrath of the War Council. They will be informed—by myself personally—of who you are and the role you're playing to bring your mates to justice. The survivors in your platoon will never know what you did until it's far too late for them to do anything. You'll be completely safe—at least once you find and subdue them for the Council operatives to collect. Your Enhancement is that you can incite animalistic rage or imbue monk-like calm with just a touch of bare skin, correct?"

Gunner nodded. Even War Thug could be made entirely docile long enough for him to be netted and taken away. It could be done, and Gunner was the only one (other than Fugly) with an Enhancement that changed targets' *will*, not overcome them with force. Entire planets of bugs hadn't been able to overcome their force, but part of that was thanks to Fugly and himself choosing key people to distract or psychologically disarm. Gunner knew that if he didn't agree to this man's proposal, his own would be the first neck under the sword. But if he *did* say yes, he was sentencing his best friends to be tortured and die in his stead.

It was like the man could read Gunner's mind: "They can't escape anyway. Everyone thinks the War Council looks the other way when it comes to resort planets, but how can anyone *really* believe that? The Council keeps a close eye *everywhere*—on places like Altair, they just do it invisibly so as not to upset the tourists. But trust me, Gunner, they—*we*—infest this whole planet like roaches after the Armada attack. The Council is doing things here that you will never know about, that nobody will ever know about.

"So, your friends are already as good as dead. There's no reason you need to die with them. There's no reason why you can't get as rich as Leo Bulero at the same time."

"But I want to *save* them. They're more than fellow soldiers. They're my *friends*."

"Are they?"

"Wha—of *course* they are! We've saved each other's lives a hundred times!"

The shiny teeth shaped into a smile. "Would you save the life of a brand-new member of the platoon, one who was assigned to your ship only the day before?"

"What kind of question is that? Of *course*!"

"Then that's duty, sergeant, not friendship." The collector in the hood went on: "Would a friend—say, your chief, War Thug—make his entire platoon suffer the consequences for something *he* decided to do, for something he then *did* do, wiping out *years* of War Council science and infuriating the command structure of the entire military? Did your commander even hold a *vote* among his men and women to do this thing that he knew would result in the ignominious deaths of every one of them?"

"Sarge always asked for input, but he also always said the *Blue Celeste* wasn't a democracy."

"Exactly. And if some of your mates agreed with his decision and even helped him carry it out, they dragged you down with them, didn't they? You weren't given a vote in your own fate. Those who went along with War Thug's plans voted for *your* demise by *their* actions. Those are not friends—those are blind followers in a cult of personality."

But ... they *were* his friends, weren't they? It might have been the extreme conditions and trauma he had just gone through, but he couldn't even remember if he was one of those explicitly agreeing with Sarge, or if he had simply silently acceded to his plan. Had he gotten lumped in with them after the Super-Nuke was set, compelled to believe that he really *was* a traitor, at least as much as the rest of them were? But this Council operative playing his employer for all the money he could get knew all of this somehow.

Holy shit, he thought. *I was set up.*

"You may be right. You probably *are* right. But one thing," Gunner said. "Let me see your face."

Without hesitation, the collector flipped back the cloth hood. The goggles had hidden synthetic eyes, unnerving gold circles with slits that shined with unfathomable coldness, and his right hand had obviously been replaced with automail. In addition, Gunner now understood why he could see the man's smile even under the darkness of his shroud: his teeth were constructed completely out of highly polished metal.

The Council collector was no one Gunner knew, no one he had ever seen before, not even with his original hands or eyes or teeth, he was sure. It was not a pleasant sight. "All right," he said, trying not to react to the visage before him, but his mind echoed faintly, *Loyal is as loyal does.*

"So we have a deal?"

"Not yet," Gunner said. "Tell me your name."

The shiny smile twitched, but the collector reformed it in an instant and said, "Of course. You may call me Mister Palmer."

"That's your name?"

"That's what you may call me. I will respond to that name, so yes, functionally speaking, it is my name." Mister Palmer extended his metal hand.

Knowing that this was as good as he was going to get, Gunner shook the cold steel—which *wasn't* automail at all, but metal the man still maneuvered like a real hand—and said, "We have a deal."

4

The tether connecting the assassin Junebug and the infantryman Fugly failed to break as they hurtled down through the Altarian atmosphere. They had to pull their chutes once it became clear that it wasn't going to break and they'd have to take their chances, hoping their whirling connected bodies wouldn't foul each other's lines and fail to arrest their freefall. Their leap gear helmets remained on, of course, but for all that they exchanged a glance of—camaraderie? hope? farewell?—and yanked the cord to release the parachutes.

The chutes caught the air, and they both felt the illusion of being pulled up as their speed almost immediately fell from terminal velocity to survivable velocity. They were still whirling around, the tether still in place, but their nanosilk lines didn't become entangled and fold the chutes out of the shape needed to bring them safely to the ground.

In retrospect, they saw that almost any other two people *would* have gotten their lines fouled and fell to their deaths. But Fugly was slim, almost slight, so that her beauty glamour Enhancement could throw a field of any diameter larger than herself (making her irresistible to almost *any* size human or Xeno). On the other end of the spectrum was Junebug's Enhancement of extreme density, which provided her with *much* more mass than someone else of her already formidable and squarish size would have.

Thus, the laws of physics saved them. Junebug was so much heavier than Fugly that the barycenter—the point on the tether that they revolved around—was about ten inches away from the larger woman. Watching them fall, it would seem that big Junebug was more or less spinning in place with Fugly looping around her in an orbit the length of the tether. But because of the disparity, Junebug's chute opened essentially vertically and normally, but Fugly's centrifugal force meant that her shoot opened at almost a 45-degree angle, slowing them less than Junebug's but contributing enough that they then fell at a nonlethal speed. Most importantly, Fugly's chute opened *out and away* from Junebug's, and so the lines never crossed one another enough to get entangled. Any other two SEALs wouldn't have had this disparity in mass and would have died, still spinning, as their useless parachutes dropped with them, at maximum velocity, to the ground.

Instead, Fugly and Junebug landed at a safe speed but were unable to plant their feet because of the inertia of their tethered tailspin. They flopped onto the ground and were dragged in a circle by their chutes until each could hit the switch to separate them. Once those detached, they stopped dragging and came to rest. If they hadn't been wearing helmets, their faces would have been scoured off by the dirt and rocks.

Junebug sat up and slid hers off. "Fugly? Fugly!" she called to the small, prone body on its back at the other end of the still-intact tether, since the comms in the helmets were not working. "Oh, goddamnit, Fugly, you—"

Her partner bent her arm at the elbow and gave her a thumbs-up. Then it flopped back down and Fugly didn't move again until Junebug was able to shake off her minor injury (as well as her end of the tether) and walk over to nudge Fugly with the toe of her boot.

"Get up, bitch, we got work to do," Junebug said with a smile. She knelt down and unlatched Fugly's end of the tether and sat her up. "You okay in there, ya ugly mug?"

Fugly laughed a little weakly and pulled off her helmet. The glamour Enhancement wasn't something she could just turn on or off—it just *was*, and the face that smiled through Fugly's pain was the most perfectly proportioned Junebug had ever seen. Perfectly proportioned, gentle if you liked gentle, naughty if you liked naughty, giant pincers and mouth feelers if you were a native of Klendathu, anything that made one want to gaze, love, bang like a drum. Fugly was a woman in Junebug's perception, stocky like herself, with kind eyes as green as the crystal rain falling on a star in Orion's sword. She wished she could—

Junebug shook herself out of the trance and helped her platoon-mate to her feet. "Everything check out?"

"Roger that," Fugly said, after patting herself down. "I feel like I just fell out of spaceship, though."

They laughed and looked around. The area wasn't deserted as such—there were small, crude buildings that nonetheless pumped out music of definite Terran origin.

"We didn't exactly land in prime real estate, did we?"

Fugly laughed again and slipped her helmet back on. She didn't want anyone to fall victim to her glamour unless it was intended just for them. In this backwater, there could be rape gangs or just plain marauders who would try to rape her because she was there. They'd probably try to cut Junebug to ribbons as well.

They'd *try*.

Against two highly trained professional killers, any attackers were unlikely to succeed. But they didn't need the hassle nor the notice, having no idea what the situation was here on the ground. With no comm, they couldn't know if the rest of the unit had been killed, captured, taken off-world, anything. They also couldn't radio in for a rendezvous.

There was just dirt and dust and rocks … and that cantina or whatever that festive little dive was a few hundred meters away.

"Any suggestions?" Fugly said, her voice barely muffled by the helmet.

"We're lucky, 'cause there's almost no one around. But we are shit out of luck 'cause there's almost no one around, y'know?"

Fugly nodded. "So … any suggestions?"

"We got some credits. They must have food and drink and information in that cantina or whatever it is over there."

"We need to get out of SEAL jump gear and into something more … I don't know, *resortish*? I have to hide my face or we'll be the center of attention. Not in the good way, either."

"It could be a trap."

"Only if someone knew in advance where we would land. Could be dangerous anyway."

Junebug shrugged her wide shoulders. "My suggestion is that we hide the chutes, then get inside whatever *that* is and lie low until we can get information on the rest of the platoon." Seeing Fugly's nod, she added, "And we can see what the War Council has in store for its new enemies."

***

As if on cue, a light antigrav Spinner hove into view and set down ten meters on the opposite side of the women, away from the cantina. The scissor doors slid up, and a humanoid climbed out. They couldn't tell if it was a human or a bipedal alien within the monkish robe and hood, but its right hand was artificial, smooth metal unlike automail but that also fully articulated. With its face covered, the figure forced Fugly and Junebug to stiffen into a barely perceptible but very real defensive stance. The figure approached, carrying a parcel under the arm on its good side.

Walking—almost sauntering—right up to the two women, the apparent human male said from under the hood , "You planning to go into the bar over there?"

"None of your goddamn business," Junebug said, positioning herself to make her seem even bigger, already much larger than the slim figure of their visitor. After a few glances between herself and Fugly, she softened a bit and said, "Okay, yeah. Not much else to do around this ass-end of Altair, I'm thinking."

The obscured biped let out the susurration of a snake's laugh. "Then you'll need these." He held out the parcel, a square of brown cloth.

"Drop it on the ground. Then back up. My partner here can end you with one chop of her hand against what I'm betting is a skinny neck."

The visitor took a few graceful steps backward.

Junebug kept her eyes on him (it?) as she reached down and unwrapped the package. Inside were two brown hooded robes, exactly—*exactly*—what Junebug and Fugly needed. "All right, what's the gag here? How did you know?"

"I know a lot of things," the shrouded thing said. "I could be of use to you."

"Of use?" Fugly said. "What makes you think we need assistance?"

"Nothing, of course. I must just be a good guesser."

"Are you a human?"

"Yes."

"Show us."

He rasped a laugh again and flipped back his hood. "Am I not an absolute vision?" he asked with a shiny smile as they took in his face.

What they saw were his artificial slit eyes, silver teeth, and—they noticed it only when he used his hands to show his face—one artificial hand that wasn't automail, but moved like it was. "I hope my stigmata don't offend you. I'm quite human, I promise. Well, most of me."

"I've seen worse," Junebug said.

"Very kind of you to say so." He looked at Fugly now and said, "Your turn. New friends need to see each other's faces, don't they?"

Fugly hesitated before slipping off her helmet. Junebug still saw the butchy beauty of her dreams, but she wondered what this man was looking at right now. Whatever it was, Fugly's face would appear as the most attractive specimen of whatever the stranger found irresistible.

"Ah," was all he said. "Well, you'll want to wear these into the bar, *soldiers*. I recommend burying those uniforms in the sand so no … *unpleasant* people find them."

"Who *are* you?"

"I'm someone who has a vested interest in your well-being."

"You don't even know who we are!" Fugly protested.

"Are you not Lieutenants [Fugly's real name] and [Junebug's real name] of the late, much-lamented *Blue Celeste*?" He smiled at their reaction, which formed his pockmarks into thin ovals. "I will be sitting in the Spinner until you come out of the cantina. That is, *if* you come out." He pulled the hood forward again, gave a slight bow to the ladies, and returned to his vehicle.

Junebug examined the robe and hood from every angle, inside and out. There were voluminous pockets on the inside, and the cloth was lightweight and allowed air to move in and out. When she was done, she said to Fugly, "I don't see anything but a robe. Looks clean."

"Then what do we do?"

"Just like Slit Eyes said: We put these on and get into the cantina, get the information we need, and then get the hell out to rescue our mates."

Fugly narrowed her eyes a bit. "Why would that stranger help us? I mean, was he even a stranger? How the hell could he know who we are?"

"He must have caught wind of our ship crashing and saw us in our leapsuits, put two and two together. Maybe he's a sympathizer against the War Council, who knows?"

"But he knew our *names*."

"Fugs, wake up—our names are on our suits, right above our left tits. He actually did us another favor, not letting us go into that wretched hive with our goddamn names printed for everyone to see. He must be telling some version of the truth about being invested in our well-being and shit."

Fugly could tell she was whining, but her head was spinning like the rotors on the disfigured man's antigrav vehicle.

Fugly sighed and said, "That makes as much sense as anything else. But we should leave our boxers and wifebeaters on under these things. Don't want rowdy, drunken folk seeing more than they need to." They both knew what she meant: anything like Fugly's Enhanced face, which they'd never forget and would pass on and on to anyone who would listen.

"Roger that," Junebug said, and they undressed, put on the robes, and together they dug a shallow grave into which they shoved anything identifying them as military.

✳✳✳

The robes hung perfectly on them, Junebug's fitting her huge frame and Fugly's her slim one. The weird dude had crafted everything as perfectly as an origami unicorn. But *why*? If he was a War Council operative, why didn't he just blast them and collect their heads? Or, if he wanted them alive for a no-doubt bigger reward, pop their eardrums with a sonic blunderbuss? That caused instant unconsciousness lasting long enough for him to bind them with unbreakable nylon—neither one of them had a strength Enhancement, so that would be game over, and they would end up in Council custody, trussed up for the tortuous termination of their short lives.

The brown cloth hid both their faces nicely, and they didn't look too out of place entering the cantina: their robes, after all, were probably standard issue in the desert area of Altair, since they both blocked the intense bluish sunlight and enabled their wearers' sweat to evaporate. A few heads turned at the bar counter or around the adobe tables, but their interest didn't last long and they looked away.

"This is good," Fugly whispered.

"Anything nonfatal is good right now." Junebug was more circumspect in her appraisal of the bar, with its live band and clientele that looked made up almost entirely of hardscrabble freighter crews and other Merchant Space Marine workers who transported goods both sanctioned by the Council and those that were not. These men and women wanted to drink, screw, and otherwise be left alone. But Junebug in her travels on resort planets just like Altair had learned there was one other aspect of low-profile cantinas like this one: The men and women on the fringes of Council control were always looking to make a deal. *Always*.

This could be smuggling anything from human beings escaped from Council detention—dealing with Xenos in any way would mean the end of their days as free men and women—to spices to crystals common on Altair but valuable beyond belief back on Terra. Generations after the epochal disaster of the Armada attack, the multiple EMPs of that War meant that the electrical infrastructure had to be built from scratch, and the effort to find EMP-proof power sources was ongoing. Crystals on the Sol system's asteroid Vesta worked very well in transmitting electricity, but the cristobalite and tridymite formations orbiting newly formed stars actually *produced* electricity in the right environment. Terra possessed that right environment, and any smuggler brave enough to enter the swarm of gems floating within these forming systems—and lucky enough to survive—would find himself with more credits that he knew what to do with if he could get those commodities back to Terra.

So Junebug knew what kind of men and women she would find there, and they were just the ones she and Fugly needed. Only by getting off-planet could they do a serious grid search for their platoon-mates, if any of the rest of them had even survived the destruction of their ship.

The two hooded figures approached the bar, and the barkeep eyed them so suspiciously both women thought someone threatening must have been standing behind them.

"Welcome to Chalmun's Cantina," he said with a smile heavy with irony. "Now show me your faces or get the drumpf out of here. Or, if you prefer, we have blasting services if you assholes decide to annoy me or my customers … or be aliens." His kept his hand noticeably behind the bar, so there was no reason not to believe he had an atomizer or worse.

Junebug slung back her hood entirely, but Fugly opened hers so only the barman could see her uniquely attractive face. He nodded sternly to the bigger woman, but a stunned look covered his face when he saw what was under Fugly's hood. "Wow," he said, his gruff demeanor sliding off like snake skin. "Excuse my rudeness—we get mostly assholes in here." He pulled himself together and said, "Come in. But a word of warning: keep to yourself, don't cause trouble. This riff-raff will slice off your face and wear it like a hat. Then they'll get serious about causing some pain."

They indicated that they understood and reshrouded themselves with the hoods.

Some of the men at the bar could have been criminals, either political or something more mundane, like murderers. The women, too, some of whom matched Junebug in girth but not in muscle. Others, both men and women, looked chronically underfed, maybe slaves let out of their chains for some break earned from their owners. Or escaped, trying to lie low until their captors tired of looking for them.

What Junebug and Fugly *didn't* see was anyone in military garb, in their whites or their khakis worn on shore leave at a resort planet. They also didn't notice anyone who, at first glance, looked like they were War Council spies. The pockmarked overdressed weirdo in the Spinner car outside looked like a Council operative, but if he was one, his actions made no sense at all.

"Maybe we'll be safe here," Junebug said quietly as they waited to order at the bar.

"If we need the crowd to protect us, I'll show my Enhancement."

"The Nuclear Option," Junebug said, and she could tell Fugly was amused. From the now-friendly barkeep, she ordered a Sullustan Gin martini, neat, for herself and an Ice Blaster (also made with Sullustan Gin) for Fugly. Gin was a girl's drink, but ordering it with a touch of vermouth and bitters was more stereotypically manly. Junebug hoped this would make the other patrons see her as a large man instead of a large woman. That was important in a fine establishment such as this one, filled as it was with crews of space freighters and whatnot who hadn't had a new human woman maybe in years.

An Ice Blaster *was* a girl's drink, but Fugly was a goddamn assassin and so just *let* somebody try to screw with her. After all, she had perfected the "grab and twist" genital removal technique, something that made Junebug cringe even though she had no junk to detach.

They didn't sit at any of tables, just leaned against the bar sipping their drinks and watching the rest of the customers. Nothing seemed out of place for a scum pit, and the clientele didn't even look especially threatening. That didn't really help them, though—they needed to get off-world to run a grid scan for their fellow SEALs, and it was difficult to discern who might be a pilot willing to take on an explicitly capital offense even if Fugly showed her face and made goo-goo eyes at him.

Junebug wasn't really sure how to ask—

"*Hey! Assholes! We need a pilot to get us off this rock, do a couple of orbits, then come back,*" Fugly shouted, projecting her voice so everyone in the entire cantina could hear her. "*We got credits. Who's game?*"

The bar's occupants were silenced momentarily by the assassin's broadcast, but before too long, murmurs and susurrations filled the room. One woman gave a slight wave of her hand to get Fugly's attention and said, "I'm a pilot. I got grid-scan capabilities, too. That's what you need, right?"

Fugly stiffened for a moment but realized that a grid scan of the surface was pretty much the only thing one would need an immediate couple of orbits for. "That's right."

"How many credits you two men of the cloth got on you?"

Fugly answered with the actual figure—you didn't need credits if you were dead. It amounted to one tour's salary, easily a third of what a Space Navy SEAL would earn in a year.

The entire bar erupted in laughter, some big and tough bastards wiping their eyes with mirth. The pilot merely smiled and said, "That's not enough to get me to skip the rest of this drink. Sorry, friend."

The bartender, still floating in infatuation from seeing Fugly's glamour, stepped to where they were leaning against the bar and whispered behind them, "You can get that money easy, ladies."

They turned, and Junebug said, "We're listening."

"They got a special … *club*, I guess you'd call it. The guys and gals here are ready to throw down serious cash at any moment to wager on a good fight. I'll pay what you need for the pilot out of my earnings."

"We get the money, win or lose?" Fugly asked.

"If you lose, sure, if there's still anything of you left to pay. But there's two of you—the animals in here would want Gigantor to fight. They like a competitive brawl to bet on. The beautiful lady would get the winnings if the big girl dies in the ring."

"So, a fight to the death," Junebug said. She'd had enough of that to last a lifetime during her SEAL graduation test.

"No, no," the barkeep said, too lightly. "You just gotta last three minutes in the ring with our champion. Three minutes, that's all. You don't got to kill it, you don't got to get killed. Easy as it gets."

Junebug and Fugly exchanged glances—they knew Junebug could dispatch any fight champ. They fought *Xenos* for a living, for chrissake!

"Make it so," Fugly said, and the bartender stepped up onto the bar and announced that they had a challenger for Rampage, the undefeated champion of Chalmun's Cantina.

"Undefeated?" Junebug said, confused. "Does that mean no one lasted in the ring for even three minutes with this guy?"

Fugly gave a little shrug. "There's more than one way not to last three minutes in a fight. One of them is no longer being alive."

Junebug cracked her sizeable knuckles and shared a crooked smile. "That's *every* fight to a SEAL, baby."

The crowd in the cantina abandoned their tables and the bar, not even bothering to take their drinks with them. They all squeezed through a door in the back. That's where the ring was, the platoon-mates guessed, and where they would earn the money to look for their friends ... as the barkeep would say, *If there was still anything of them left to look.*

* * *

After making it down the rough steps into the basement, they entered an almost airless room now filled with rowdy degenerates hungry to see something bloody. Fugly found a place along the adobe wall, and Junebug went forward toward the "ring," a shallow pit dug in the middle of the room. It had reinforced adobe—or maybe concrete, or putty-covered metal—lining the walls of the pit from its base and extending about a meter past floor level. This allowed the ghouls in attendance to see the fight without the combatants eyeballing anything except each other. Where the adobe wall ended, metal fencing stretched all the way to the ceiling. There was no one yet on the inside of the fence.

The barkeep was still taking credits and giving slips of paper as receipts, so Junebug turned her attention to the ring. It was pretty much square, maybe twenty feet on a side, and the floor as level as anything else in the building. She couldn't see how she could get into the fighting space, however. There was a square on the floor that looked like a big trapdoor, but that would mean coming up from some lower level. She imagined someone would clue her in so she could fight. She was down to her boxers and wifebeater. No gloves; this was to be a bare-knuckles brawl, apparently.

She was right about getting clued in: the bartender and another large man each took hold of a rough rope handle on the outside of the adobe ring just where Junebug was standing—she hadn't even noticed it—and pulled out a section of wall. An audible click made it clear that this was a door that locked.

Way to go, Ace, she thought, and felt a twinge at the thought of her missing comrade.

But there was no time for lamenting right now. The two men pulled away a six-foot section of the wall, and if it was made of baked mud and clay, then it had to be reinforced with some serious iron rebar to weigh as much as it looked like it did. They set it down with just enough clearance for Junebug to bend over and pass through before they lifted, slid, and locked it into place again. Inside the ring, it came up to about her knees.

The crowd was slightly elevated, then, in place to see all of the action, and they cheered and booed in equal measure. Junebug wasn't just massive and muscled, with a density Enhancement that made her *very* hard to move or resist once she got moving—she was also trained extensively in hand-to-hand combat, how to murder with her hands and feet, as all SEALs were. Her fellows in arms were the toughest, the most aggressive toward their enemies, and the most used to killing things until there were no more things on a planet to kill.

"Hey, Big Girl!" the barkeep and now bookie shouted at her from just the other side of the chain-linked metal. "C'mere and I'll tell you the rules!"

Still alone in the ring, Junebug stepped over.

"Once it comes out, I start the timer. It's accurate, don't worry; the sons of bitches taking the long odds don't want you in there one extra second. It counts down to three minutes. If you ain't knocked out cold or dead at the end of that three minutes, you're the winner."

That all sounded right, except … "Once *it* comes out?"

"Sssh," the barkeep said, an index finger over his lips. "If the Council finds out, we'll *all* be miners for life."

"Whoa, finds out wh—" she started to say, part stern and part panicked. She touched the metal fencing to talk closer to him and

POWWWWW!

was thrown onto her back near the center of the ring, stunned and twitching. The fence was electrified; she should've figured. She was feeling less confident about her chances of winning against an *it*—whatever the hell that meant—with no way to get out of the goddamn ring to surrender or just plain escape and forfeit the match.

She could now hear some creaking and clanking down under the trapdoor. Her eyes sought out the still-cloaked Fugly, who must have been standing on a table or chair near the back. There was nothing Fugly could do. There was nothing *Junebug* could do.

The trapdoor burst open, and the crowd went completely wild. Junebug whirled around to see what climbed out of the lower level, and for the first time in her tough life, she *screamed.*

Not ten feet away from her, sniffing the air with its twitching feelers, was an Archeron Crab. It had not noticed Junebug yet, and she remained stock-still. Her mind reeled: the Archeron Crab *did not exist*. It was a chimera invented by military textbook writers to portray the most vicious Xenomorph a human could possibly face. In those books, the creature had the elongated head of the military-bred, nigh-unkillable "attack alien" that was tried in the field but almost immediately withdrawn and destroyed. The problem was that it went after human forces with as much enthusiasm as it did the Xeno enemies.

But the Crab—this impossible thing *now right in front of Junebug*—was like that "attack alien" crossbred with a scorpion, all jagged exoskeleton and six legs plus two "arms" up front with massive pincers on the ends. The pincers were bound, god knew how, so that they couldn't squeeze and slice her in half. It didn't seem to have eyes as such. Was it blind? Maybe that was to make the "fight" more interesting, or possibly to keep it from killing its handlers, whatever idiots they were? But that hardly mattered—the Archeron Crab could kill you a hundred other ways, especially if you were without a weapon. You weren't going to kill it with your hands and feet, no matter how well trained you were.

The military textbook in which this thing was described recommended one course of action if a platoon faced this half-bug, half-sentient alien: *Get to your ship and nuke it from orbit.* There was no resource on any planet infested with Archeron Crabs that would be worth fighting these monsters, even with railguns, even with neutron concussion grenades, even with any weapon humans had created or even devised. The Archeron Crabs quickly massed wherever they scented prey and overpowered their human opponents even when multiple platoons were sent to face them at the same time.

Advantage Junebug: This was a single Crab. Its pincers were bound. It couldn't see.

Advantage Killer Alien Crab: Its poisonous saliva and acidic blood, its tremendous strength and impenetrable exoskeleton, the huge poisonous barb at the end of its curled tail, and its rows of teeth that looked like metal knives meant that it would probably kill her in five seconds, let alone three minutes.

But it had to find her first.

The Crab sniffed the air for another moment—Junebug was damned glad there were so many space rats down here yelling and screaming and smelling like none of their ships had been equipped with sonic showers—and opened its metal jaws to pierce the entire room with the sound of fury. That shit didn't just look like metal—its teeth and jaws *were* metal.

How the hell did this get bred? Junebug's mind spat, and then she realized that humans weren't the only creatures in the galaxy that could be Enhanced. The Crab's metallic mouth was no more natural or unnatural than Junebug's inhuman density.

Then it lunged. It leaped at the place where Junebug had been standing only a second before, her scent apparently lingering. Perhaps feeling that she had to be very near, the Crab swung its pincers through the nearby space, narrowly missing Junebug, but her luck was going to run out soon if she didn't get her ass on the offensive *now*.

But where to strike? The Crab had its back to her—well, the back of its thick tail—Junebug searched for some spot where she could at least give the goddamn thing a *cramp*. She spotted the countdown clock. Barely twenty seconds had passed. Could she dodge the thing for another two and a half minutes? No. *No.* She had to hit it hard and then get out of the way, keep it off balance—

UNGHH! The massive tail came down on her shoulder, something that would have flattened a non-Enhanced person of normal density but still made tears of pain shoot out of this Enhanced-density person. The funny thing was—*ha frickin' ha*—

that this wasn't even an attack move by the Crab. It was just searching for its enemy and moved its tail. That was all.

It didn't even need to attack to kill. But it spun around on its many legs and attacked anyway: it swung a pincer and hit her hard on the side of her body. Junebug yelled in agony, but her mass kept her from being knocked down or even rocked. In fact, the Crab pulled its pincer back in apparent pain.

I can do this. She looked at the timer. *Fifteen more seconds down. Just keep moving, make sure its blows are ones you can absorb.*

The Crab recovered from its shock quickly, and when it went after her again, the crowd was whipped into an even greater frenzy. Catching her scent anew, the Crab threw forward its tail and poisonous barb. The corrosive toxin hissed into the basement floor, sizzling in the spot where it punctured the surface, just a foot away from Junebug, who fell on her ass and scrambled backward in near-panic until she reached the wall.

Not knowing what else to do, she hugged the wall in her sitting position. The Crab sniffed the air once more, trying to pinpoint where she had gone. But it seemed the creature was at a disadvantage: having sensed her height when it had slapped her with its pincer, it now flung its appendages in that height range, whipping each one right above her head.

She tried not to breathe. She wished she could get her own scent off of her. The Crab was perched over her now, sniffing at the crowd, getting confused. If she could have gotten up and taken a run at the horrible thing, she might have knocked it over, or at least made it lose its balance. But she was trapped, inches away from death, right in the shadow of this alien beast.

It took another sniff—and its head whipped down to instinctively "look" at where it perceived her to be, even though its eyes were gone. Almost seeming excited, it backed up, two black petals falling from its face—

—and then it really *did* look at her. It hadn't been blinded. The fight organizers must have covered the thing's black, merciless eyes with some kind of patches that it couldn't shake off, that would only pop off at the handlers' radio signal or whatever they used.

She looked at the clock. *1:50.* She had yet to land one blow on the Crab. The only pain or injury it had suffered came from its own attacks on her. And now that it could *see* her... The bastards running the fight must have kept it blind for a short time just to keep the playing field level. That would help the bets balance out even a little bit as the crowd thought it was more of an even match than it would be as soon as they handed over their credits.

But that window was closed now. It was too close to use its pincers as blunt instruments, so the Crab extended those metal jaws and teeth to reach her and tear off anything it touched.

Junebug was pinned against the wall. There was nothing she could do, watching those knife-edge metallic teeth drip gelatinous saliva as they came toward her.

Wait, the thought reached through her terror.

Those are metal.

In an instant, her body moving even before she consciously realized what she was doing, she launched herself with as much force as she could manage and slammed her lead-dense head into the bottom of the Crab's jaw while kicking at its front legs behind the pincers. Her scalp tore open against the ragged Xeno and blood poured down her face, but that didn't mean anything. The momentum behind her impact shoved the Crab's head upward and the loss of its stance made it fall forward, its wet metal teeth slamming into the electrified chain-link fencing.

The crowd had heard it roar with fury and shout with pain, but they'd never heard the Archeron Crab scream in terror and agony. Smoke rose from its jaw, which was galvanized against the charged metal.

Then there was a low whirring sound and the sizzling stopped. The Xeno was able to tear itself off the fencing, even though it was obviously still stunned.

A quick glance revealed that the barkeep had flipped the huge switch that electrified the cage, no doubt trying to keep the Crab winning and to avoid having to pay out odds of 1,000 to 1.

The crowd went into an infuriated frenzy when they realized what had just happened. One burly son of a bitch punched the barkeep right in the nose, and the crunch could be heard even in all the noise. Then the burly man shoved the big switch back into place—the hum of electric current immediately filled the room again, noticeable only after its absence—and stood guard in front of it. The greedy bartender was conscious, but his nose was mashed and leaking blood at an alarming rate. He raised a slim whistle to his mouth and blew on it—*oooo-EEE-oooo*—snapping the Archeron Crab out of its electrified daze.

That certainly got its attention, Junebug thought, and shook out of her own daze as the Crab started after her again, this time with plenty of room to puncture her with its barb, knock her senseless with its pincers, bite off her arm—or her head—with its jaws, whatever it wanted to do. Her scent didn't matter now. There was nowhere in the ring to hide for the next minute and twenty seconds. She managed to get just past its offensives, but blood was streaming into her eyes from her torn scalp, and her energy was starting to flag. The Crab seemed to sense this and slowed down as if enjoying every step it took toward its injured prey. Ten, fifteen, twenty seconds ticked by. There was no way the Crab could have been timing it to kill her just as the buzzer went off, but the suspense was killing the onlookers, and soon the monster would be killing *her*.

Junebug wished right then that she had a different Enhancement, something like Leonard's light show or Dahlia's unbreakability. But there was no point in—

Oooo-EEEEEE-oooooooooooooooooo!

The sound came from the back of the room, from behind the Crab, and it turned simultaneously with everyone in the crowd to see a hooded figure standing on a chair with the barkeep's whistle somehow in her hand, held up to her mouth. Fugly whistled again, making sure every eye in the house was on her, and sloughed off her robe. Her undergarments were gone. Every man, woman—and Archeron Crab—in the room saw what to them was the epitome of loveliness, the most precious, the most ethereal of priceless beauty.

The Crab stood in awe, just like everyone in the room, and gazed upon Fugly's glamour. It had turned from Junebug and stepped forward toward its angel, not pressing against the electrified metal but close to it. Saliva cascaded from its teeth as it almost seemed to want to kiss her.

Finally, Junebug could make her offensive move. She had the size of a 250-pound shotput thrower, all large muscles and fat to give them cushion. But her mass made her more like a pre-War combustion-engine automobile, a big one, like a Caddy-Lack or a Hum-V car-tank. When she built up speed, then—even over just the fifteen feet of a fighting ring—she delivered a momentous impact like one of those gasoline cars running full-speed into a police roadblock. (Junebug enjoyed vids of late-twentieth-century action movies.)

She lowered her shoulder and drove that momentum directly into the ass-end of the Crab, shoving it forward and its conductor-coated metal teeth right into the re-electrified fence. It screamed and tried desperately to pull itself away from the cage, but it was galvanized to it, unable to separate itself, and dense Junebug remained at the base of its tail, where none of its many ways to kill her could get at her.

The sparks flying from the Archeron Crab's mouth danced across the ring and into the crowd. Finally, the fence shorted out and the Xeno fell to the floor, motionless, but still breathing. The illegal creation wasn't going to die just because it had gotten a massive dose of electricity shot through its body, apparently. That made Junebug immediately start looking to get out of the ring.

Then a couple of things happened at once: The buzzer sounded, and everyone who had taken the long odds cheered like maniacs, moving en masse to the luckless barkeep for their payouts. Fugly swooped her robe and hood back on, again obscuring her features. But some of the men—and women—in the room could not control their intense lust and came at her. The assassin broke their necks those of five more overly libidinous assholes before any more attackers decided to get fresh.

And Junebug jumped with all her weight against the fried—and thus more brittle—area on the fence where the Crab had gotten its knockout portion of electron juice. She crashed right through the fence and pushed aside anyone who got between her and Fugly and then the door.

These assholes get entertained by watching people die? Junebug thought as she hustled Fugly out the door. *Then this should just kill them.*

She slammed the basement door shut and not only threw the bolt but also laid one of those heavy adobe tables at an angle under the handle. Before she pulled the door closed, however, she saw the Archeron Crab stir inside the now-open ring. It was waking up.

The cheers behind the door soon turned to screams, but every second there were fewer and fewer until the last one was replaced with the wet sounds of flesh being rent, chewed, and swallowed. Not wanting to be there another second, Fugly and Junebug made a beeline for—

"Close one, eh?" the lone figure in the room called to them, making them both yelp in surprise. It was the ship captain, the one who had laughed at their offer earlier. "You must be some kind of fighter to get out of that pit alive, Biggie."

Junebug's mouth was agape. "You *knew* there was a Xeno down there—a goddamn *Archeron Crab*—and didn't say anything? The failure to report *any* alien is a capital—

"Yeah, yeah, a capital offense. That's pretty rich coming from a couple of ex-SEALs on the run. Besides, what *doesn't* get you a death sentence from the War Council these days?" The woman tipped her chair back, placing her boots on the table. "You'll lose your shit in a week if you worry about following every new rule the Council makes. Anyway, you two happen to grab any cash on your way out? I seem to remember that being a factor in you going down into the basement in the first place."

"We were a little busy trying not to get killed or raped," Fugly said.

The captain laughed. "You must be pretty good-looking, then, 'cause nobody's gonna rape *that*," she said, redundantly pointing at Junebug. "No offense, Biggie."

"You'll know when I take offense. It won't be pleasant."

"Hey, hey, let's all be friends here." She tipped her chair forward, stood, and extended her hand to Junebug, who (why not) shook it, and then to Fugly, who (what the heck) did the same.

Friends now or not, Junebug was stern: "How do you know who we are? What we are?"

The captain smiled at that and said, "Your friend from outside, the guy with the metal hand and the artificial eyes? He came in and told me while you all were downstairs having your party."

"*Palmer*? He came in while you were here, alone?"

"Yeah, I never was much of a fight fan. Damned glad now, too."

"*No*, I mean, why did he come to *you*?"

The smug captain pulled out a wad of credit notes from inside her cleavage. "To give me this. Enough money—*more* than enough money—to get you two where you need to go," she said. "Anyway, enough small talk. I'm Captain Mallory. I own the nine-man transport ship *Tranquility*, docked out back."

"I didn't see anything docked anywhere."

"Exactly."

"Is it a fast ship?" Fugly asked.

Mallory looked sincerely surprised. "*Fast ship*? You've never heard of the Sandfly-class *Tranquility*?"

"No," the two women said as one.

"Good. That's how I like it. We smuggle 'spice,' and I don't mean paprika. We also have been known to relieve other transports of the burden of their cargo now and then."

"You're a bunch of pirates," Fugly said with unmistakable disdain.

"No, no, we don't hurt anybody. We have some defensive weapons and such, but we don't capture the crews and deliver them to slavers or any of that bad juju. Nah, we do it just for the money, and those corporate haulers are insured anyway."

"Oh, I take it back then," Fugly said dryly. "You're just a bunch of assholes."

Mallory laughed heartily at that, leaning back with arms akimbo. "Right you are, small fry. But listen, you two are paying customers—or customers who are paid for, or whatever—so we'll get you where you're going without hassling you too much." She clapped Junebug on the shoulder, and they both laughed.

Fugly didn't join in the merriment. "Captain, what do you mean, 'where we're going'? We just want to do a grid scan to find our, um, *friends*."

"Yeah, your friends? You wouldn't by chance be referring to the rest of your crew of traitors who crashed here?" She looked at the eyes beneath their hoods. "Your metal-mouth benefactor didn't mention a grid scan when he handed over the cash."

Fugly tried to catch Junebug's eye—*did everyone on the planet know the* Blue Celeste *had come down?*—but to no avail. So she said, "Well, that's what we want. Can you do it or not?"

Mallory said, "Grid-scan equipment comes standard with Sandfly-class vessels. Don't you worry—if they're down here, this ship can find them. I assume you have their chip frequencies? Should be the same as yours, only with two unique identifier symbols at the end."

Through the hood, Junebug slapped her forehead. *That's how that odd man knew where to find us!* They were all chipped so that the Council could send rescue crews if they were in a crash or got stranded on a hostile planet. The chips were passive—they responded to search frequencies but otherwise did no transmitting. Because they were so small, they would register a detectable response only when the search frequency was sent from fairly close by.

Like from on a resort planet.

"Can you read the chips?" Junebug asked, feeling very exposed all of a sudden.

Mallory said, "Only the War Council is allowed to have the technology for that."

"Goddamnit."

"Luckily, the *Tranquility* was in War Council service before I bought it, and I guess I just forgot to take the chip scanner out," she said with a smile. "I like being an asshole."

Junebug allowed herself a smirk. "You're really good at it."

"High praise." She squinted out one of the small windows cut out of the adobe wall and twisted her lips in thought. "Listen, it's getting dark, we won't be able to fly until morning."

"What? Why?"

"The Council knows every beacon of every vessel on Altair. Moving at night is considered suspicious, to say the least." She looked at each of her two hooded companions. "I don't need any extra suspicion pointed my way, do you?"

They didn't. So they would bunk down with the captain and crew and hope they would be off to find their mates as soon as the Altair system's sunlight touched the *Tranquility*.

5

Leonard was dead.

Hog didn't know what had killed him, but when Hog awoke in the middle of the night, the tether between him and his mate was no longer connected, and even just the starlight showed a crumpled parachute not a hundred feet from his own landing spot—crashing spot, actually—as he had been knocked out cold. He felt like he had hit so hard he must have left a crater, but he'd broken nothing, despite a bruised soreness that seemed to permeate every cell of his body with pain.

He picked himself up and unlatched his chute. He walked toward the other, crumpled pile of nanosilk, wincing with each step. "Leonard! *Leonard*! Wake up, man, we got ourselves a new world to conquer!"

But nothing stirred at his mate's landing spot.

"Leonard, buddy, get your ass up! If *I* can do it the way I feel right now, I *know* you … can …"

Just a few yards from the parachute was an automail arm. With no one attached.

Oh, no. No, no, no. Goddamnit, no.

Another *no* sounded in Hog's brain with each movement he made, the *no*'s cadence in sync with his throbbing pain and, now, his throat seizing up with grief and foreboding.

"Leonard?" Hog lifted the nanosilk up and out of the way, and there was Leonard, motionless, twisted in a way that was not possible for anything but a corpse. "Aw, Leonard, don't. Don't. *Don't* …" he muttered, tears falling, as he knelt down on the rocky ground to touch his mate of more tours than he could remember. He turned the body over and immediately saw what had killed him, and it wasn't the fall.

Leonard was barely recognizable through the charred flesh of his face, and his leapsuit had been burned off his body—Hog was sure it was him by his missing right arm, the one made of automail. It must have been torn off on impact to end up where it was now.

It was the nose cone—Leonard couldn't control the unknown current on a system specifically designed never to be tampered with, had never done an EVA, and was burned to death *from the inside*.

Hog had no implements to dig his friend a grave in the hard ground. So he did all he could: he wrapped Leonard's body carefully in his shiny parachute and carried it to a space between two nearby boulders. He laid his mate down, stood straight, and saluted him. It was too dark to see his body from a standing position, and that was good. *Leonard* was good. He wasn't a traitor to the War on Alien Aggression, and now he wouldn't have to bear the hatred of Terrans pumped up by Council propaganda, shouting horrors at him while he stood in the docks and was sentenced to be publicly tortured to death.

But Hog would, if he couldn't lie low long enough to figure out where his platoon-mates had been flung to—or if they were even alive. Hog was a powerful fighter even without his vibration Enhancement, but if the others were all gone, he didn't know if he had it in him to fight just to remain alone.

The darkness of whatever canyon or plateau he had landed on—he couldn't see enough to know which it might be, or something else entirely—gave him a sense of peace to fight off his sadness at Leonard's death and fear of what might be waiting for him at the end of this misadventure.

He carried Leonard's automail arm, not knowing why but maybe as a way of making amends for not dying with him. He marveled at the artificial limb's lightness. As he walked, he occasionally shifted the arm but kept it tucked under his own arm after he absentmindedly stuck his thumb into it and it immediately started trying to attach itself to his living flesh. He pulled his thumb out in seconds, but that hurt like hell, yet another pain to enjoy as he tried to find his way on Altair.

He was a strong-backed Space Navy SEAL, so he could march until the sun came up—in fact, that's what he planned to do, if you could call that a plan, exactly. He didn't know the asterisms in this sector, so he didn't know if he was heading east or west, north or south. He would consider whatever direction this system's sun appeared to rise in as "the east." He was the dumbest lummox on the *Blue Celeste*—he called himself that, and it was fine because you didn't need a PhD to end the existence of a planet full of Xenos bent on humanity's destruction. But even still, he was smart enough, and enough of a space traveler, to recognize certain stars were in different positions an hour after he had started walking. He was heading "west," then, so the Altair sun would rise behind him.

It wouldn't rise in the direction he was facing, but after another hour's march, there was a definite glow along the horizon. A city? Maybe this was going to be some of the famous resort planet luxuries? Would he be able to find the rest of the crew? Hope sprung up in him, and he kept marching at a steady pace, the aches and pains now just spurring him on.

When he looked up to keep track of the star as a way of measuring the time passing, he noticed that at twelve o'clock but at about a 45-degree declination from the zenith—in other words, a spot he could keep in his field of vision as he walked—was a flying car. A Spinner, if he was identifying the pattern of lights softly changing hue and frequency correctly. It looked to be about a thousand feet in the air, matching his marching speed almost exactly. After realizing this last, he knew it *had* to be a Spinner, because nothing else of that size was able to move so slowly and remain airborne. The company kept the antigrav technology a secret—except from the War Council, of course, who would use it in many ways, but building stylish passenger vehicles was not among them.

He didn't have any idea how deep into nighttime it was on the patch of Altair he was walking on, but it looked like he would reach the source of the artificial light in no more than two or three hours. If he was correct that the Spinner was trying to guide him, he wondered, why didn't the driver just land and pick him up?

No matter. It was nice to have the company making sure he got to the right place. He unclipped the water bottle from his suit and drank deeply. Someone in the city would know what had happened to his platoon. Maybe the person in the Spinner somehow knew, and that's why he was guiding Hog.

He just hoped that whatever had happened to them was not "the War Council."

6

"Rise and shine, assholes."

Sarge was already as cleaned up as he could get without his shaving kit and a change of clothes. We were veterans of survival training in places worse than even the ass-end of Altair, so we found some edible roots and even water before starting out toward the now-barely-visible smokestack effluvium. After Sarge had tentatively identified its source as some industrial facility, I was unable to think of the vapor or smoke as anything other than the discharge of smokestacks. Altair wasn't Terra, not by a long shot, and so its manufacturing or whatever the heck it was a few miles ahead of us could very well still be using smokestacks. Actually, if that proved to be the case, that would be the most helpful sign we could receive about which way to point our boots.

We walked in silence for almost an hour before Dahlia said what must have been on her mind all morning: "Sarge, what if the Council does try to take us? What if it's not just operatives or whatever, but Space Navy and Army troops? How do we engage other soldiers with instructions to eliminate us with extreme prejudice? Do we kill them?"

Sarge had a pebble in his mouth to keep his saliva going, but at this he spit it to the side and stopped our march. "Sailor, this is a goddamn pickle I never thought I'd see. If these other military members, men and women in uniform fighting against the alien menace, have been ordered to hunt us and kill us on sight, that don't mean we have an obligation to stand still and take it. I'm gonna be the first to run and hide in a pit, if that'll make the difference between getting holes opened in me where they don't belong and *not* getting them.

"Cowardly? Maybe. But that's how it goes when a soldier is hunting treasonous personnel—sworn soldiers have to follow what their commanders tell them, or else *they're* traitors, too.

"But *us* killing these soldiers told to hunt us when they haven't done anything but loyally follow orders? You assholes all know that I love to kill, I *live* to kill, but I cannot and will not raise a gun or pull a knife or even punch an honest grunt sent on a miserable mission. I'll *protect* myself, *protect* my troops, but I'll kill *myself* before I just went after a man or woman following legitimate orders.

"In this case, I ain't afraid to die. It's just part of a soldier's oath. But I'm afraid to *kill* for no reason. My reason for living is to kill enemies, but fellow soldiers? I do that, I'm no better than the filthiest bug out there. And that's all I got to say on the matter."

Dahlia and I were silent for a moment. "Quite a speech," I said at last.

"Yeah, I'm the goddamn Cicero of the Space Navy." He took a long look at both of us, waiting. Finally, he barked, "So, you assholes gonna share your deep and tender feelings?"

"I won't do it," Dahlia said. "If I can't get away, I'll surrender. Or do what Sarge said." She made her fingers into a gun and mimed blowing her brains out.

Now it was my turn, and I told the truth. "I don't know what I'll do until I see those rifles firing at me. Right now I want to say, *No way, I wouldn't shoot at my own people*, but sir, Dahlia … I really don't know what I'll do. Maybe I'm a coward."

"Secure that, Boswell. Your whole life can't be labeled because of one battle, or one moment of self-preservation. You're a SEAL, you're elite, but you're human. And you have guts, we've seen that time and time again." He put his hand on my shoulder like a father would. "Now, let's go find out what you'll do."

It was a moment, I won't deny it. It gave me strength and made me firm in my resolve to do what was right in what we had all decided, without realizing it, was going to be a showdown at the facility we were now within one hour of reaching.

We started our march again, each of us lost in our own thoughts. I didn't think Sarge was right, in one particular aspect: This battle, ambush, whatever was about to happen, it *would* define us, for the rest of our long or very, very short lives to come.

***

At daybreak, Fugly and Junebug rose stiffly. It wasn't until they heard the crew moving around that they grokked the *Tranquility* was about to lift off.

Fugly said, very quietly, "How are they going to grid scan without us telling them the frequencies?"

Junebug answered, "Maybe they need to reach a certain altitude first." But she was suspicious, as any former law-enforcing soldier would be, of being at the mercy of a ship full of pirates.

"What coordinates, Cap?" the extensively pierced and tattooed pilot—they *were* like pirates—called from the cockpit.

Captain Mallory shouted back from her seat near their passengers a series of numbers that Fugly and Junebug, knowing nothing about Altair's longitude point of origin or how far or near they were from it, had no chance of understanding. If they *had* known the place that the coordinates referenced, they might have tried to force their way off the ship before it could leave the ground.

As it was, they weren't two minutes in the air before they simultaneously realized that there was not going to be a grid scan. The *Tranquility*—and everyone inside—wasn't doing anything except going to the coordinates given to Mallory. The change of plan might have had to do with her being paid enough cash to fill the space in her considerable cleavage.

It didn't take long, flying into the rising run, for them to reach the place specified by those coordinates, a massive crater almost entirely taken up by a multi-segment megabuilding with three smokestacks puking god knew what into the air they flew through.

"Captain," Junebug said with as much control as she could muster, "what the shit is going on here? You shanghaied us—you kidnapped us—you were never *going* to do a grid scan!"

"Relax," Mallory said. "Mister Palmer paid good money for me to bring you here. If he had bad intentions, why would he waste the credits? He could've just blasted the both of you before you even came into the bar."

"I could kill you with two motions of one hand."

"I could kill you *much* more slowly, and you'd look at me like I was your own personal angel," Fugly said.

Mallory waved them off. "I know, Space Navy SEALs, very tough, kill more beings before breakfast than most soldiers do in a lifetime, so on and so forth. But if you killed me, I've got eight tough-as-brass-balls crew members who you'd have to deal with."

"Then we'd—"

"Yes, you'd kill them, too, probably very easily with your set of skills and Enhancements. But for all your wondrous methods of murder, you don't know two things that are very important to you right now."

They waited, not wanting to give her the satisfaction of their curiosity and fear.

"One, you don't recognize the tactic of stalling; and two, I'm betting that neither of you knows how to pilot a Sandfly-class transport vessel." She beamed a smile at them. "That little bump you just felt would be this ship touching down."

They shot glances out the viewport. It was true.

Goddamnit.

"So, it's too late for heroics now. Out you go."

The hatch opened, and two of the muscled crewmen pulled them up—well, pulled Fugly up; Junebug was unmovable as a mountain until she watched Fugly get pushed out the door and had to join her mate. Before she stepped out, however, she turned and jabbed a finger at the captain. "You'd better hope I never see you again."

Mallory seemed unfazed. "It was nothing personal. I like you two spunky chicks. It was purely business. Maybe *we'll* do business someday, who knows?"

"I do. The War Council will have us strung up before the sun goes down here. And that's only if we're lucky."

The captain did seem a bit sad at this. She said with remorse, "At the end of the day, us pirates can only care about what coin we make. Sorry, soldier."

Junebug nodded, less furious and more resigned now. As she stepped down the platform, a half-dozen men and women in tan uniforms and private-issue blasters rushed past her and into the *Tranquility*. She almost turned back, but at the end of the day, what happened to pirates was none of her business.

Once outside in the crisp air, Junebug joined Fugly, and they moved toward the humongous complex. What did they make here? Resort planets weren't supposed to have any industry at all, let alone some gigantic manufacturing complex.

Junebug was getting really tired of resort planet Altair.

They went toward the glass doors on the side of the building, but before they reached them, the doors opened to reveal a businessman so well-groomed and dressed that it took a moment to recognize his burning eyes, his Archeron Crab–like metal teeth, his false hand.

"Mister Palmer," Fugly said with deep disdain. "Of course."

Junebug shook her head like she couldn't believe what she was seeing. "*What the hell*? Why did you send us here with those assholes if you were going to be here anyway? Are you a goddamn psychopath?"

"More of a sociopath, really. Believe me, I know what I'm doing." He said this with that inhuman smile as the women joined him, still in the brown robes he had given them outside the cantina, and they walked down a perfectly polished corridor that didn't have a single door or window in it. "Also, the Council doesn't appreciate pirates disrupting trade, disrupting the efficient flow of goods and humans that keep us safe from new alien aggression. Killed two birds with one stone. Kind of proud of myself, really."

Junebug was the one who felt some remorse now.

Fugly said, "Those operatives with the blasters—they're not Space Army or Navy, are they?"

"No, indeed," Palmer said. "They are private contractors not fit for the rigors of space warfare, but just right for in-house Council security forces."

"Wait," Junebug said. "This … *whatever* this is … is part of the War Council? There's not supposed to be any industry at all on—"

"I know, I know. That's why it's so perfect. No one is going to say a damned thing about seeing this monstrosity in the desert, because then a lot of unpleasant questions would be asked in some most unpleasant ways about why the individual in question was 'taking interest' in an illegal operation in the first place."

Fugly and Junebug exchanged a glance. *We know it's a Council operation now.*

They came at last to the first door they had encountered in their long trek down the hallway. "This is it," Palmer said, and motioned that one of them should open the door. "You're about to hear what all the ruckus is about."

There was nothing but to do it. Junebug put her hand against the electrostatic control and the door slid open. Inside the room was a conference table, potted plants, a pitcher of water. And several people sitting in chairs, eyes open but unfocused, bodies limp but upright.

It was Inman, Killshot, and Gunner, plus Miss Symantha's captives Opperman and Presto. Inman looked like he had been hit and run over by a dozen land tanks. Killshot was bloodied, with one eye swollen shut. Gunner didn't look much the worse for wear, but still looked like shit, anger somehow showing even through his slack features.

"What in th—" was all Junebug could get out before her hood was whipped back and a jet-injector forced a cocktail of chemicals through her thick flesh and into her bloodstream.

Fugly didn't even have time to turn, let alone run, before a second hand threw back her hood and injected her as well.

Not fully awake, but not totally unconscious, either, the two SEALs were led to their chairs at the table, to drool and stare with their comrades from the *Blue Celeste*. Four chairs remained empty, but Mister Palmer and Miss Symantha weren't worried. The others were on their way.

7

Neither War Thug, Dahlia, nor I had Enhanced vision, but none of us could miss the staccato repetition of reflected glare from the long metal object, its carrier shuffling in the dirt in a way that looked tired even this far away. We were practically at the rim of the crater when it became obvious that the burdened pilgrim was headed to the same place as we. Another hundred steps from our group and from this lone stranger brought us close enough together to see who it was.

"Hog!" Dahlia cried, and this stone-cold infantryman ran to him like a husband greeting his wife after she returned from a long tour in the Oort Cloud. Hearing and seeing who it was, Hog gently placed the metal piece on the ground and then ran to meet her in the middle. Their wallop as they met might have shaken the ground under our feet. Wrapped in each other's arms, they shared as long a kiss as they could without it becoming a burden to Sarge's mission.

"I did not see that coming, sir," I said.

"Heh. Must've been smoldering right under our noses forever, but they're too good of soldiers to break the concentration of our platoon. None of that shit matters now, except *Lovebirds, let's get moving*!" he shouted at them, and we all laughed as Hog picked up the thing—an automail arm, I could see now—and they double-timed it back to us.

Sarge threw his one arm around Hog's neck and man-hugged him good while I slapped him on the back. When our leader saw what Hog had with him, however, the smile fell from his face. All he said was, "Leonard."

Eyes closed, Hog nodded. Then he handed the metal-scaled limb to Sarge. "But his automail came off in the impact. I thought maybe you could use it."

Sarge nodded now, too, and said, "Good thinking under duress, Hog. Let's see—"

He didn't finish his sentence because when he placed his stump into the automail, it immediately started entangling itself in Sarge's nerves and muscles, ultimately securing itself to the humerus of his right arm.

This automail had been to replace Leonard's entire arm, and while our unit tech was tall with long arms, Sarge was taller with longer and much bigger arms. So it looked a little comical when the artificial arm finished fusing to Sarge, a full arm attached to the elbow of his lost arm.

He flexed the new arm, twiddled his fingers. "Maybe this keeps Leonard with us a little longer, guys."

We all smiled at his comment, but it was hard not to get choked up.

"Also, this extends my reach by two feet. That's not good for the bad guys," he said, and laughed, making us laugh with him. "Oh, wait, that's *us* now. In that case, it's not good for the good guys!"

There were four of us now, half the surviving platoon, and we moved as one to the edge of a depression in the ground that held what we finally saw was a massive factory.

Sarge was right: Those really were enormous smokestacks reaching up from the center of the massive facility toward the turquoise morning sky of Altair, spewing dirty vapor and smoke into the air. But there was no reason for the pollution to exist: nothing was being built or processed in any military-industrial sense. The smokestacks were, literally, a smokescreen. They were there so it looked like something real, something good, something in support of the War on Alien Aggression, even if that wasn't technically allowed on a resort planet. But it wasn't anything good, and each of us learned that as we converged—or were herded—to this place.

I now understood why, as we got near enough to the facility to see the shadows in the billowing vapor, we weren't able to view the actual complex of buildings itself. It resided on the flat bottom of an ancient meteor crater, its smokestacks barely even breaking the plane of the terrain surrounding the huge depression.

There was a path to the bottom, so we took it. We were almost to the perimeter of the hot-laser invisible fencing, something that would have sliced us into cold cuts had we walked through it. That's when a man wearing a uniform and pointing some kind of plasma rifle at us came out of a small structure on our side of the laser fence and yelled at us to stop.

We stopped. I'm sure Sarge, Dahlia, and I all were thinking of our conversation on the way to the crater, seeing the business end of a rifle held by a husky man in uniform. But I also saw—and could practically *feel* Sarge and Dahlia seeing—that the khaki uniform was that of a War Council contractor. It made no bones about it, either: it had the worker's name ("Purvis") emblazoned above the left pocket and "War Council Support" above the right. "Stand back *right now*." He was belligerent from the get-go. Great.

We all held up our hands—Sarge with one real arm and one automail arm reaching a full three feet further up—and tried to look as nonthreatening as possible, no easy task for a Space Navy SEAL. "We don't want any trouble," Sarge said.

The stout man kept the rifle trained on us, but he didn't seem to know how to hold it correctly. Plasma rifles don't ricochet, but you can burn the side of your own body off. "Then what *do* you want? You are trespassing, and I have permission to use deadly force against invaders. This is a protected facility."

Protected from whom? I thought, but kept it to myself.

"I think you know what we want," Sarge said. "Don't tell me you don't know who we are."

The man stared at us long and hard, but absolutely no current went to any lightbulb above the angry Purvis's head. "I'm going to call in for instructions. You move, I blast you." He sounded like he was hoping he would get the chance.

We each shrugged, amused at our synchronized response that seemed to just further perplex this independent Council contractor.

He spoke into a mic on his lapel, turning away from us so we couldn't hear what he was saying. Normally, this would have been the stupidest thing in the world to do, as any of us could have broken his spine with a hard kick from our boots. Or, less severely, we could have pulled a weapon on him and made him drop his. However, the contractor's confused demeanor was almost funny. *Almost*—why the hell did the War Council have a manufacturing facility of some kind on a planet where it had itself expressly forbidden such activity? It could have built it on any of the hundreds of now-empty alien worlds we had cleansed of potential enemies.

Maybe it would have attracted too much attention anywhere else. Maybe doing this on a resort planet, where it was operating in plain sight (from the right angle), was a way of ensuring it would be left alone by people not wanting to have anything to do with such an obvious violation of Council decrees?

The worker turned back around, his private conversation ended. We knew it was good for us because he didn't raise his rifle at us again. He stepped to a console inside the little shed and shut down the hot-laser barrier of the section we stood at. "You morons got lucky. I described you, and they said to let you in. They told me to tell you that your friends are already here."

That took us by surprise. "Our friends?" Dahlia said, knowing the answer as she asked, "What friends?"

"Hell if I know. They don't explain jack to me about what goes on in this place, just who to let in and who not to. Now let's *go*— get out of my face." He shut off the hot-laser fencing for us to pass. Dahlia, Hog, and I all passed, but Sarge stayed behind on the other side. We guessed he wanted to talk to the guard a little—

Whack! Sarge plowed his new and unbreakable automail fist into the back of Purvis's head, knocking him down and grabbing the guard's plasma gun. Without hesitation, he pulled the trigger and *ZAP*, our erstwhile helper's head was reduced to a little pile of smoldering goo.

Sarge was smiling—his first kill since Planet Bunghole—until he saw the rest of us, shell-shocked at his actions.

"What? He wasn't military!"

Once again, I felt sure his Enhancement was killing. But that was our War Thug.

"Besides, we need that fence *down* if things get FUBAR in there and we need to make a quick getaway."

"Always got to keep options open," Hog said.

"And our eyes," Dahlia said.

"What a clever bunch of assholes you are," Sarge said with a smirk, then got serious again. "Troops, we're gonna rush those glass doors in front, get inside, and do a room-by-room check."

"Roger," we each said.

"*Now*," Sarge ordered, and we immediately made a tight formation, going serpentine and switching places continually in case any snipers wanted to get cute.

"Our friends," Dahlia said. "Our platoon, he must have meant that."

"Why would they be *here*?" I said as we walked toward what looked like the front entrance of the huge campus of buildings. "What *is* this, anyway?"

Sarge said in a low voice, "Let's just focus on getting through the front door, troops. I get the feeling we'll have answers soon. Like, *real* soon."

Sarge wasn't wrong. As we approached the double glass doors, they opened to reveal a civilian in a crisp pinstripe business suit standing in the middle of a polished lobby. His shoes gleamed, the floor gleamed, everything gleamed exactly as the interior of a filth-spewing factory wouldn't.

"Welcome," Mister Palmer said. With the morning sun reflecting off his machine-vision slits and silver teeth, he looked like a man literally filled with fire.

***

"You are [Hog's real name], the one, very unfortunately, they call 'Hog'?"

"That's me, motherfrakker."

"And [Dahlia's real name], you are the 'unbreakable' one, correct?"

"Name: [Dahlia's real name]; rank: Lieutenant; serial number zero-five-nine—"

"Yes, yes, that's part of the Space Forces rules, but you're not a member of the Space Navy anymore, are you?" His teeth made him look like a robot shark in human clothing.

Now he looked at me. "Lieutenant Boswell, I presume."

"Correct," I said, maybe slightly more curtly than absolutely necessary.

"A lot of former Lieutenants on the former *Blue Celeste*, no, *Mister* Boswell? What is that, the lowest rank a SEAL can be and fight in the field? Not terribly ambitious."

"Eat my shit," I said. "And do it slow, I want you to savor it."

My compatriots chuckled, and the golden-orbed slit eye cracked an ironic smile. Now the man actually left his place on the shiny tile and walked right up to Sarge. Our commander was a good head taller than this weird man in the pinstripe suit, but no intimidation registered in his demeanor or his speech.

"And now we have the famous 'War Thug,' the killing machine. You have single-handedly—pardon the pun—brought entire planets of Xenos to extinction. I mean you and your platoon, but *you*. The cream of the crop, now a king without a country."

For his part, Sarge didn't rise to the man's taunts. "We just want to retrieve our platoon-mates and leave … whatever the hell this place is. I don't care who you are or how you got us all here—"

"It was rather clever, if I may say so—"

"I said *I don't care*. Just shut that bear trap of a mouth and take us to them. It'll be much more pleasant for you if you do it right now." Sarge gave him a smile I sincerely hope will never be directed toward me. "It'll be much more pleasant for *me* if you don't."

"I hate to ruin your bloodbath dreams, but I'll take you there *right now*, as you say. I'm Mister Palmer, by the way."

Sarge looked at me as we followed Palmer. "You remember anything from the data banks on this jerk-off?"

I entered my mind palace and quickly retrieved what I was looking for, even though it was an article I had barely skimmed ten years ago. But there it was. I said quietly as we walked down a long, long corridor, "He is a super-rich industrialist. His eyes and mouth and right hand were replaced after he crashed his private spacecraft on Pluto. And … Sarge?"

He indicated for me to continue.

"He must *own* this place. Nothing in the documents I've seen says so, but he has that kind of attitude, if I may speculate, sir."

Sarge just nodded acknowledgment as we came to the only door near the end of the long corridor.

"Here we are," Palmer said. "Your compatriots are inside."

"Like to know how you got them here," Sarge grumbled, almost inaudibly.

Palmer showed no reaction to War Thug. "We rescued them from all around Altair, picking up each individual or team and shuttling them back here for medical treatment. I warn you, they might seem a little groggy from medication, but they will understand if you talk to them, even if they can't yet respond."

"Something smells awfully fishy here," Sarge said. I agreed but kept my own counsel.

Palmer smiled, which was more unsettling up close even than it had been from ten feet away. "You may judge for yourself," he said, and opened the door and stepped back, next to Hog, who was the last in our little line, allowing us to pass into the conference room.

It wasn't until later when I debriefed the other survivors that I understood what happened next: Before we had taken one step, Palmer had out his concealed jet-injector and silently took out Hog, Dahlia, and myself, finishing each of us off before Hog even went limp and hit the deck.

War Thug spun around as soon as he realized something wrong was happening, but they were planning on that; Miss Symantha jet-injected him in the back of the neck, an extra-large dose for this extra-large man.

Miss Symantha and Mister Palmer smiled at each other. It was almost *too* easy. Symantha called for her two lugs, Dark-hair and Blondie, to drag the semiconscious quartet to the empty chairs and make them as comfortable as possible for what was about to happen.

8

Slumped in my chair in the conference room, I watched things happen in slow motion even though I could tell everything moved in normal speed. I don't know what they injected us with, but it was like pouring syrup on my consciousness. I could understand everything that was said, could feel emotions about it, even think of responses, but I remained motionless and couldn't focus my eyes, let alone talk. I was sure my platoon-mates were in the same condition, but I couldn't move my head to see anyone else.

"Welcome, friends," Mister Palmer said from the front of the room, toward which we were all more or less pointed. "I'm very sorry for the inconvenience of tranquilizing you, but I didn't need a group of Enhanced ex-soldiers on the run to liquefy me or set me ablaze with their eyes or what have you.

"I've brought, stolen, or coerced each of you to come to this facility. In doing so, I have been able to keep the War Council happy, because they don't want to unnerve the resort planet visitors with some show of force. It's much better for them to send an operative, what they call a 'collector'—that would be me—to round up you ladies and gentlemen and gift wrap you for them to pick up in an everyday-looking small transport vessel. Then, as you all know very well, they would take you back to Terra—or Earth, whichever you folks prefer—to torture you to death not only on every Terran broadcast, but also on galactic subspace vidreels. As a warning, of course, to not mess with the War Council, especially not destroy a planet in which they had invested so much time and so many resources.

"It sounds like I'm a villain 'monologuing' in some second-rate vid, doesn't it? But I'm not the villain here—I'm the hero, the one who unleashes the forces of good to battle evil. The good news is that we *do* have a villain. The bad news is that it's … wait for it … *the War Council*. Shocking? No. They are ruthless, endlessly deep-pocketed, and have the full support of the Terran public. Maybe through fear, maybe through real patriotism, but if the Council says you're traitors or enemies of the state in the War on Alien Aggression, then the public will call you traitors and then call for your head."

He paused. "The Council wanted my new pharmaceutical line, because it could be mixed in with cities' repaired water lines."

Somebody managed to slur something. Palmer took that as asking what the drug did.

"It was a recreational drug, really. A kind of hallucinogen from the Prox system that I bought the exclusive rights to. But what it did was make hallucinations feel real and the real world feel like a mist of fluctuating hallucinations. I don't think they've ever resorted to using it on the population, but I bet they would if enough people cottoned on to the truth about the 'War on Alien Aggression.' They wanted it, I wouldn't sell, and they shot my ship down onto Pluto, then proceeded to remove important parts of my body, one by one, until I capitulated and gave them the drugs and the notes on how to grow the lichen. I couldn't resist any further when they cut out my eyes."

"Shit," Inman kind of said.

"With my money, I could get them replaced, but with the Council wanting me blind, toothless, and one-handed, it was all I could do to get these repulsive stigmata." He sighed. "In any case, I have a fine, fine assortment of weapons close to hand that are so illegal on a resort planet—hell, so illegal in *any* Council-claimed system in the galaxy—that they wouldn't even bother to torture me. They'd just vaporize me on the spot.

"But I need you guys to kill for me, murder, destroy." He looked to Sarge. "Sounds good, right, War Thug? You killed that poor sap at the gate, but that didn't satisfy you, did it? No, there's *so* much more killing for you to do. Now, who's excited?"

I was more angry and nervous than excited. But I was also anxious to know what could be going on that was so horrible that a fantastically wealthy man would risk everything, including his own life, to put an end to it. Since Palmer obviously wanted to *badly* hurt the War Council and we all had been brought here, my money was on the destruction on this very facility. It looked like Terran factories, had to be a manufacturing venture of some kind. The best guess I could make was that they made superweapons here, maybe even something more powerful than the Super-Nuke, although that was hard to even imagine.

Maybe it was a different kind of manufacturing. Like creating the next generation of fighting men and women. Were they cultivating new super-soldiers here, using what they learned from the late scientists on Planet Bunghole before we brought that enterprise to a sudden end? They *did* seem to be just perfecting their technique there, using SEALs to fine-tune their grisly business of making soldiers into slavering monsters.

It boggled my drugged mind to even think how many obscenities of science could be "grown" at once in a place of this size and secrecy. Did they still use SEALs and λ-560 Berets for the seeds? Or was there a system of making people vanish on Altair, those on the outskirts of the law whom the Council knew wouldn't be missed? After our experience on Planet Bunghole, I wouldn't put anything past the War Council. It would commit atrocities to create new war material as long as that made the people of Terra pliable and controllable. Consolidating power for power's sake alone.

"So. Everybody ready to see what goes on here? I guarantee it'll leave you speechless … I mean, if you could speak right now," Palmer said, supremely self-satisfied. "Miss Symantha?"

A slinky raven-haired woman possessed of a cold beauty so intense it almost hurt to see sashayed into the room, looking as out of place in this corporate environment as a Busho haiku in a textbook on Spinner repair. "Hello, troops," she said with a white-toothed smile. "Thanks for coming."

Palmer laughed. "Now, I know our Miss Symantha has tortured some of you to compel you to join our team. There's little as motivating as the threat of decades of forcible sodomy, right, Lieutenant Inman? But let's leave all that behind us as we move on with our mission. I believe you'll find that you can walk now, albeit without complete bodily freedom."

Dark and Blond and a clutch of uniformed Council contractors entered, each with an unbreakable-looking pole with torso loop on the end.

"Please rise, troops."

We must have all wanted to test what our bodies could do, because we certainly didn't stand up as one to follow Slit Eyes' orders. The lackeys, unafraid of the raw power in the room since it had been sedated out of us, attached the nanocarbon loops around our torsos, locked them into place, and could then push around whatever captive they were assigned to with great ease.

"Prepare to be pissed," Palmer said. "Prepare to destroy."

What in the *hell* was he talking about? I would find out, along with our whole contingent, in just a few minutes.

9

We were led by Palmer and Symantha and pushed by the people I was already thinking of as "henchmen" through another long corridor and then down several levels. Then we entered what seemed like a huge pipe, a passage that was wet and slimy to enhance the effect.

We must have walked for half an hour. None of us had any idea where we were, and as our minds cleared and (more slowly) we regained control of our muscles, I don't think anyone would have turned on our keepers yet for fear of being lost to thirst and starvation, even if we did have the strength and weren't at the end of those goddamn poles.

At the end of the pipe was an enormous hangar that looked like it could accommodate a Constellation-class starship. We were led out on a catwalk—Symantha must have changed her shoes—and were just high enough that I couldn't really tell what the maze of walls below was supposed to be. I looked at Killshot, who could see what they were with his Enhanced vision, and saw that he had lost all color in his face. His lip quivered.

Oh, what in the goddamn galaxy does he see?

"Blitzen, bring our man Presto here, please," Miss Symantha said to Blondie. His name was *Blitzen*. I would rather have gone by "Blondie," personally.

The former magician was brought to her and his loop removed. He didn't look terribly strong—quite the opposite, weak with hunger and probably torture for Symantha's amusement—and so Palmer and Symantha obviously thought he was no threat. What was he going to do, make their rabbit disappear?

We had all been maneuvered to the side of the catwalk to view what was going to happen. The maze below looked like it was maybe transparent aluminum, definitely see-through, I could tell from its more distant walls.

Killshot vomited down the front of his tattered leapsuit.

My body was coming back to me now, and I could feel myself quaking at the thought of what Killshot could possibly have been seeing.

"Presto," Symantha said, "You were the first traitor I ever brought on board. I knew the general outline of what I wanted to do, and I thought maybe your skills at prestidigitation would be useful. I was wrong. But you *are* still useful, don't worry.

"Blitz?"

The blond took two steps and shoved Presto right over the railing. Presto screamed all the way down, and even though he had to be mortally injured from the fall, upon landing, he remained alive, conscious, and screaming.

Palmer spoke up from his relaxed, cross-armed lean against the other railing. "Let's go down a couple of levels. You guys are going to *love* this."

We carefully made our way down the metal steps against the wall and then down and down until we exited onto another catwalk, this one much closer to the mass of horrors below.

An air horn sounded and some old-fashioned spinning red alarms started up. Symantha literally rubbed her hands together in anticipation. "Three," she breathed. "Two. One. *Go!*"

Obviously, as a veteran Space Navy SEAL, I've seen a lot of carnage and terrifying shit. But nothing in all my tours was like this.

Symantha yelled the countdown and when she got to *Go!* there was a sound like a thousand chairs scraping on wood floors. Then they rushed out, hundreds, *thousands* coming out of what I could tell now were individual cells with transparent walls.

The rest of me came back in a rush, and out of my mouth came the scream, *"What the drumpf are those? What the holy drumpf ARE those things?!?"*

Junebug and Fugly answered as one, sounding small and nauseated: "Archeron Crabs."

No one asked them how they knew. I don't think any of us *wanted* to know.

Inman said, "Those aren't real—they're mythical, like centaurs, *god, oh, god …*"

They were each as large as a bull, as black as a pit, as—

The first six-legged monsters to get to Presto immediately tore him in half with their massive pincers. It stopped his screaming, but not ours. Every one of us watched the Crabs—more like giant

Xeno scorpions, with the metal teeth and huge stingers of the monsters kids (and SEAL trainees) read about in scary books—flood over any scrap of Presto they could reach, looking like river fish swarming over a tossed piece of bread.

I finally puked. So did Junebug. And Fugly. And Inman and Killshot and poor shaking Opperman.

"Those," Mister Palmer said plainly, "are what the Council has been growing here on Altair."

I think the only reason that the now-functioning War Thug didn't pull Palmer's head off right then was because there was no way to get your head around what the man was saying. Not *implying*—flat-out stating as a fact.

I *did* notice, however, that both Mister Palmer and Miss Symantha had pulled away from our group and were holding boomsticks between themselves and us. "Don't get mad at *us*, troops. *We* didn't have anything to do with this. We're just trying to put a stop to it. The War Council is making these monsters for a *reason*."

Assuming that everyone was as thoroughly confused as I was, I tore my attention away from the Crabs—who were desperately trying to climb the walls or the tops of their former cages to get at us—and said, "What possible reason could there be for *this*? We risk our lives every goddamn day to *kill* these pieces of shit all over the goddamn galaxy!"

My mates gawked in surprise. That's not my usual way of talking.

The only sound for twenty seconds or so was the snapping and snarling of the Archeron Crabs and the scratching of metal in their attempt to get to the catwalk. As I often did, I looked to Sarge to try to glean what his supreme military mind was pondering.

This time, I couldn't tell. Couldn't even guess. So, as the keeper of the log even though there was no official log to post, I asked him: "Sarge, what's going on? What are you thinking?"

Sarge looked down at me like he forgot I was there, like he forgot there was anything in the universe except himself and the frenzying Crabs below. His face was pale, like Killshot's was when he first saw what was inside those cells. He noticed me now and seemed to come back to himself.

"Sarge?"

"There's gonna be a new invasion. The Council's gonna take these and let them loose on Terra. On *Earth*." He spoke like he was in a dream, or a nightmare, from which he could not quite wake. "The War Council is breeding the most deadly Xeno, the strongest, the hardest to kill, and then they're gonna unleash it on humanity."

My eyes must have goggled at his words. "W-What? They send us all over the galactic arm to *kill* Xenos, entire planets of Xenos, to protect Terra! Why—*why*—"

"Blitzen, Donner, unloop our friends," Symantha said with confidence. "They'll behave if they want to understand what's going on here."

The blond and the dark-haired thugs did what they were told and, using the poles, removed the control loops from each of us. The instant his loop was off, War Thug grabbed the loop and drove the other end of the attached pole right through Blitzen's abdomen. He screamed and gagged on blood, of course, but his real trouble came when our commander used the pole to lift and then hurl him over the railing of the catwalk. He fell into the mass of Archeron Crabs and barely had the chance to scream before he was reduced to a pulp the Xenos sucked off of one another's shiny bodies.

Symantha and Palmer looked mildly disturbed but kept their boomsticks pointed at us. If they exploded just one of them, we'd all be burned so badly we'd beg for death. So War Thug didn't go for them, instead grabbing Donner—*ho ho ho!*—and with just his hand and automail hurling him to the ravening aliens.

"Are you finished?" Symantha asked casually.

"Yes," War Thug said, a gleam in his eye.

"Good. Now I'll explain—"

"But I ain't!" Hog yelled and put one hand on each of two of the contractors … and *vibrated* them. They shook at such a frequency that, when Hog stopped, they stood in place, insensate. If they really were without their senses, so much the better for them, because Junebug grabbed them both around the neck and threw them down to the increasingly excited Crabs. "Who's next?"

The rest of the Council contractors dropped whatever they were thinking of doing and *ran* back up the catwalk.

"Smart," Inman said. "Now, go on, you sadistic bitch, tell us what you want us to know."

She tipped her head in his direction, as if thanking him for a particularly nice compliment. "Don't mind if I do." She held up her boomstick. "We're not going to let these go quite yet, but when you hear what Mister Palmer and I have to say, we won't need them."

"I'm counting on you thinking that," Dahlia growled, literally shaking with righteous anger.

"Just listen," Symantha said calmly. "There are one thousand, seven hundred, and twenty-eight Archeron Crabs down there. Some remain in their transaluminum cages because it's too thick with other feeding-frenzied aliens for them to get out and join the fun. When twelve times this number have been hatched, the War Council is going to use the automatic 'flying saucers' they have built and stored in a deep, *deep* chamber in Earth's moon and drop two of these unkillable things in each one. Then, those saucers are heading right for all of the major remaining cities of Earth."

"I killed one," Junebug said. "Me and Fugly."

Palmer displayed his horrible teeth in a smile. "Most people left on Earth—the vast majority, I should think—do *not* have pseudo-magical Enhancements, and these Xenos won't be attacking inside an electrified cage. Many, *many* people will be killed before the War Council reestablishes its benevolent sovereignty and 'saves' the people of Earth. They'll win the love of a grateful planet once again."

Killshot raised an eyebrow. "Did they stop ever being loved? We kill every alien on every planet, moon, or asteroid we can reach."

"No, you don't get it. The population of Earth hasn't suffered an alien attack in more than sixty years. Most humans alive now—including you guys—were born *after* the Armada was defeated and the War on Alien Aggression began. They're starting to think of forms of government other than a military dictatorship spanning this entire sector of the galactic arm."

Symantha broke in: "The War Council doesn't exist to protect anyone or anything. They torture and murder their subjects—and that's what all humans are, *subjects* to a government that does whatever it likes under the pretense of being the only thing standing between humans and the aliens that want to exterminate them."

"So, this is political?" Gunner said. "You're starting a revolution, is that it?"

"From the inside," I said. "You both are working from the inside to bring down the War Council."

Palmer shook his head. "Sorry. You guys are the heroes. You erased L-22233 because they were taking good men and women and making them something horrible. You killed them all, but you *saved* them, didn't you?"

Sarge said, "For all the good it did us."

"Well, now's your chance to do some *real* good."

"How's that?"

"Kill these things. *All* of them," Palmer said, indicating with his chin the churning mass of impossible alien exoskeletons. Symantha looked at him in surprise but shrugged it off quickly. He tapped one of his golden slit eyes. "I've got everything documented right here. My 'eyes' are cameras that go into my brain, and any camera can be made to record if you have the means to create the medium."

"You got the means," Sarge said.

"Damn right, I do. The Council didn't *steal* my magnificent hallucinogen so much as force me to *sell* it to them. And I've used more credits than you can count setting up this vidshow. I'm going to watch you fight these monsters, and though you might die doing it, even *that* will show that the Council wants every iota of power possible *and will kill billions of the people they're supposedly protecting* to get it."

The Archeron Crabs were getting restless, and the chomping and scratching was turning to shrieking at us on the catwalk, jumping with their powerful legs and tail to try to get at us. They were so heavy and tough, they didn't get close, but they had definitely fixed their attention on us tasty humans up here, all 1,728 of them. "I'm gonna ask you one question. Answer it right and we might be able to help you, since the War Council has decided we ain't friends anymore," Sarge said to Palmer, but also looked at Symantha as he spoke. "Answer it wrong and I'm gonna personally kill both of you, right here, right now. All right?"

I saw Symantha's eyes go briefly to her boomstick, as if she was making sure it was actually still there or if she had missed something.

"All right," Palmer said, and, without a wasted motion, tossed his boomstick at Sarge, who didn't even look at it, let alone pick it up.

Inman and Killshot and Dahlia and Hog and Fugly and Junebug and I all looked at each other like someone had just lost his mind, not sure whether it was us or if it was Mister Palmer.

"I assume you're saying that if I answer this question 'right,' however you mean that, then you will *not* kill us?"

"No guarantees," Sarge said.

That made Palmer laugh and made Symantha look like she was going to set off her boomstick as a preemptive measure and then run like hell. "What's the question, War Thug … if I may call you 'War Thug'?"

"Don't care," he grumbled. "My question is *How in hell are we supposed to kill two thousand giant Xenos?* We've got Enhancements, and we got muscles, but *one* of those goddamn things could take out all of us. All you're going to vid is a very fast massacre."

"I think you'll like my answer. Come with me, War Thug." He walked down the catwalk the opposite way that we had come, punched a code into a console to open the door on that wall, and stood aside while it slid open. "This is my answer."

Gunner's jaw dropped. As our gunnery sergeant, he was no stranger to powerful weaponry, but he said, very much out loud, "*Sweet Jumpin' Jovian Jehoshaphat.*"

The room Palmer had opened, just the part we could see from our location on the catwalk, was stocked full of big, *big* guns. Some looked too large for one person to lift; others just looked scary. I hadn't ever seen any weapons like these, and I didn't even know what they *did* yet. Apparently, Gunner, who left his position, walked past Symantha and her boomstick, and expressed his astonishment and admiration in person to Mister Palmer, felt the same way. They talked shop for a minute, then we all were called over to see what we had to fight the mass of Xenos with.

Automatic rifles loaded with plutonium rounds. Shock grenades shot out like bullets and which would stick to the exoskeletons of the Xenos before exploding. Our familiar hydronium railguns, but jacked up by a factor of four. Looking at the weapons and not down at the Xenos, it was less hard to think we could survive this. Well, if …

"Mister Palmer," I asked in my most polite tone, "are we killing the Crabs from up here, or do we have to go down there? They're so fast and so huge—and so many—that I doubt I could get five rounds off."

"No, by all means, shoot from up here. Watch for recoil—it could snap this walkway into pieces if you don't absorb it correctly—"

"We know how to use weapons," Gunner said.

"Of course, of course. There are just a lot of things that could go wrong—"

"FUBAR," Gunner corrected.

"If course, whatever you folks call it. You could end up down there, that's all I'm saying."

"*We* could?" Dahlia asked. "Where are you going?"

Palmer pointed to a high ledge, big enough for a man to stand or sit on and vid all of the action. Apparently, he had a way to get up there.

"Ah," she said.

"Let's get to it, then. I'll just go ahead and leave the armory door open if anyone wants refreshments," Palmer said, but was stopped in his tracks by Miss Symantha, now looking at him with wild eyes and her deadly boomstick pointed right at his unnatural face.

"Wait a goddamn minute, Palmer," she said, unnecessarily. "Our deal was *not* to kill every Crab. This is *my* operation now, or will be when the Council scurries away from the shitstorm and abandons and denies the existence of this facility. I greased the palms of I don't know how many War Council assholes to get you into running this place. Those Xenos are *mine*. I paid for them, goddamnit."

"I'm sorry, Symantha. I'll reimburse you every cent—"

"*No!* This operation is the last one on Altair that I don't control. I'll make more exporting these vicious bastards to security forces in fifty systems in one month than all my whores and casinos and guns earn me in a *year*."

"I can pay you more, my dear. You'll be wealthier than ever—"

"*Listen to me!* This isn't about the money. It's about me finally being the alpha *boss* of this lousy planet! It's …"

As Symantha berated Palmer, Dahlia very slowly and casually moved to stand next to Palmer. She was right in front of Miss Symantha, but the woman holding the boomstick didn't even seem to notice her.

"… and I get what I *want*, Palmer. Do we understand each other, or is this going to get really ugly?"

Dahlia chose that moment to make her move, slipping quickly between the boomstick and Mister Palmer's face. The sudden movement must have spooked Miss Symantha, and she reflexively pushed the button.

POW! HISSSSS!

The boomstick burned Dahlia's face off in an instant, the concussion of flame blocking Mister Palmer from the weapon. She fell to the grating of the catwalk and stayed there.

"*Why the hell did you do that?!?*" Hog screamed and tried to get at the woman, who seemed as shocked as anyone that she had just set off the explosive weapon. Gunner and Sarge held him back, and after they whispered something in his ear, Hog calmed down. But still, he pointed at her and said angrily, "You're damned lucky, lady. *Damned* lucky."

If Symantha looked dazed before, now she looked as perplexed as if everyone around her was suddenly speaking Coeurl. She picked up Palmer's boomstick and held it out in front of her as she made her way backward toward the door we had come through. "Look, sorry about your friend, but *nobody* is killing a *single* Crab, all right? I had Palmer bring you people here to help me *move* them to markets light-years away from here. These things will never make it to Earth, I swear to you. We're selling them far, far away, but everybody will know who runs Altair IV—*me!*"

She was almost pleading now, having just about reached the door and the control panel there. "I don't even know how these things reproduce, so these are the only Crabs there will ever be, all right? This is the jewel in my crown, okay? These are my Xenos. I paid for them! *These make* ME *the boss of this planet, not the goddamned War Council!*"

"No one cares who 'runs' this place but you, my dear," Palmer said, waving her off like an annoying insect. He took a few steps and stopped to say to Sarge, "Fire when ready, War Thug, all of you. I'm going up to vid your victory. "Get these bugs killed, and you'll be heroes again. Also, I'll pay you more than you can imagine and send you places even the War Council won't think to look. Thanks to you guys, they'll feel this kick in the nuts as the first shot in a new—*human*—war." He vanished through the door and a moment later appeared on the high platform and, smiling, trained his eyes on the bloodshed to come.

"*You want to fight these Crabs, do you?*" Miss Symantha screamed from the control panel near the opposite door. "*DO YOU?!?*"

None of us knew what she was getting at … except Palmer, who lost his smile as he yelled to us: "*Don't let her do that!*"

But we didn't know what we were supposed to stop her from doing. By the time she yanked down the cover of the control panel and mashed its huge central red button, it was too late.

10

A cacophony of air horns and sirens and flashing lights and rotating lights sent the Crabs into even more of a frenzy than they had reached when the fresh meat had been thrown down to them. And when, seconds later, the main hangar door opened—the facility must have stretched under the rim of the crater and down to where this sub-sub-basement level opened up to level ground— every Xeno's elongated head turned to see ... *freedom.*

I have never seen such big creatures—or, hell, small creatures—move as fast as the almost two thousand Archeron Crabs did when that hangar opened up to the outside. They didn't just run; they *leaped* like giant fleas, they *scampered* over one another like enormous silverfish, and yes, they *ran* faster than a Spinner can *fly.*

Symantha laughed like she had completely lost her mind.

Dahlia stood up, wiped the dead, burned flesh off her face, and stomped toward the mob boss while the rest of us were preoccupied with how unbelievably quickly the entire hangar-full of black, six-legged, two pincered, scorpion-tailed aliens washed out the giant door and spilled out onto the surface of Altair. When Dahlia got to Symantha, being an assassin, she knew exactly how much force to use to kill her with a single punch to the face.

She used just a hair under that. Sadly, Miss Symantha would miss the conclusion of her grand adventure.

By the time Dahlia returned to us, every single Xeno had cleared out of the hangar.

"Good work, soldier," Sarge said, "but we got a situation to deal with. Everybody grab as many weapons as they can carry."

As we made double-time down the catwalk and through the hangar to follow the alien horde, I caught one last look at Mister Palmer. Even that far away, I could see that if he still possessed human eyes, he would be crying.

As long as Palmer drew breath, the War Council would never be secure from his wrath. I wished him a very long life.

***

"What now, assholes?" Sarge barked when we got out into the midday sun. There were tracks where the stampede of Crabs had run, but that's all we could see of them.

"It won't take them a day to reach the resort areas," Killshot said.

"We don't have a ship, not even a Spinner," Junebug said.

"If they reach the populated areas, it's as good for the Council as if they were dropped on Terra," Fugly said.

"*Earth*," Sarge corrected. "Our planet is *Earth*."

"Aye, sir," she said. "Earth."

"We need a ship," Junebug reiterated, but there was absolutely nothing in sight. We didn't even know how far from the crater we were. By the time we got to where the Xenos had gone, there would be nothing left to save. And the brand-new War on Alien Aggression would be launched.

Everything was lost. As a SEAL, you never say that, don't even *think* it. But I was an *ex*-SEAL, and I thought the hell out of it.

Everything was—

The rush of air above us, which blew dust into us from every direction, was accompanied by the sound of a souped-up but *old* set of engines assaulting all our senses at once. The ship—a civilian vessel of some kind, I could see as I squinted into the sun—hovered above us, with what looked like five figures rappelling from an open side hatch.

"What the hell?" Sarge was surprised enough to blurt, and that didn't happen much.

I looked closer. Those weren't rappellers—those were *bodies* hung by their necks.

A head poked out of the hovering ship and shouted, "*Junebug! Fugly! Need a ride?*"

"Friends of yours?" Sarge said to them with a smirk.

"They are now," Junebug said, and yelled up to the woman that *hell* yes, we all needed a ride.

The *Tranquility* set down right next to us, kicking up dust and crumpling the five bodies under the weight of the spacecraft. The captain—Captain Mallory, as Fugly introduced her to all of us—cut the cords loose that had been around the necks of the five Council contractors who had rushed into her ship as soon as she landed inside the meteor crater.

"They had no respect," Mallory said, and that was that. "So, where can we take you, various rebel scum fighting the Council's empire?"

Killshot explained the entire situation to her—well, a shortened version without all the drama laid out, but every part including the rampaging Archeron Crabs given in fine detail.

"I *thought* you all had an awful lot of shiny weapons to just be sightseers," she said with a laugh, and called up front to her pilot, "You get that?"

"Roger, Cap. Shall we?"

"Indeed!" she said, finger pointed in the air. Then she said to Junebug and Fugly, "There's more to these pirates than coin, ladies. Not *much* more, mind you, but just enough to help out some friends."

The *Tranquility* was built for spaceflight, not just in-atmosphere flight, so it moved like the devil himself. Before five minutes had passed, the herd of insanely frightening aliens—even to think of them now is nightmare-inducing, and it is my Enhancement and my curse that I can never forget *anything*—were in sight. Thirty seconds after that, nine Space Navy SEALs, true SEALs whether we were earning a paycheck or not, had secured themselves to the open hatches on both sides of the versatile smuggling ship and trained our megaweapons on the stampede.

Plasma bolts and invisible laser blasts, high-speed hydronium projectiles and those rapid-fire sticky grenades, explosive bullets and hotly radioactive shells smashed and blew up and inverted and decapitated and burned up from the inside whole waves of the giant scorpion-looking bastards. We knew how many there were—*exactly* how many, 12^3 to be *really* exact—and we knew we had more things to shoot at them than that. But they were only fifty clicks or so away from the soldier-friendly whorehouses and casinos, and what Miss Symantha had said before her night-night time was true: If the image of these impossible Xenos overflowing a supposedly ultra-safe resort planet got to Earth, it would imbue the War Council with as much fresh power as if the Crabs had been made to look like a second Armada.

I couldn't believe the noise of all the weapons going off in an enclosed space, and immediately I thought everyone would go deaf in seconds, but I saw now that everyone had their ear protection on, and when I felt my own ears, mine was on as well. Had I forgotten that I put it on? Had I *forgotten*? But then I saw one of the crewmen of the *Tranquility* pointing at his ears and giving me a thumbs-up. He had casually saved us all from probably permanent deafness.

I liked these pirates. Except for the actual pirating part, but that was being a bit snotty. We all had to do what we had to in this time of War. Maybe fake War. But as long as the Council kept up its propaganda and scheming, a time of War it would remain.

The whole time I was thinking this, I was mowing down Crab after Crab after Crab, sometimes switching weapons when the one I was using got too hot. It was probably true that shooting an Archeron Crab with a railgun or throwing a grenade at it wouldn't kill it, might not even stop it from dispatching you with thoughtless ease. But I saw now that not even these monsters of myth made corporeal could resist the superweapons with which Mister Palmer had provided us. He may have been trying to cry back in the hangar, but seeing Miss Symantha's (and the War Council's) precious killer babies getting sliced in half with nuclear grapeshot, blown into shell fragments with those handy sticky grenades, and shrinking and shrinking in their ranks would have made him cry with joy, I bet. The War Council that had stolen his humanity was taking its lumps after all. Palmer *was* a hero in his version of this story.

The desert-edge casinos were just in sight on the horizon when we were blasting the last of the Crabs, the buzzer about to sound as we dunked the last shot. Everyone on the *Tranquility*, crewmen and military alike, let out shouts of victory as we pulled up and away from—

"*Aw, hell!*" Killshot cried. "There's still one down there—it must have been right below the ship!"

"On it," the pilot responded, and we swung down toward the lone Crab running full speed toward the heavily populated area.

But when he swung the ship to get the bastard where we could shoot at it, the damned Crab changed tack to run exactly beneath the *Tranquility*, in its very shadow.

"It's too late," Junebug said from a distant place. "People are going to die. The Council will—"

"Screw that!" Captain Mallory yelled, and ran up to the cockpit, where the pilot quickly switched control of the ship over to her. "Everybody hold on. Or don't—this is gonna hurt no matter what you do!"

No one knew what she was talking about, but our sudden stall and drop made anyone not belted in or holding on to something—which all the crewmen were, I noticed—go into zero g's for a second before the belly of the ship *whomped* onto the ground, throwing everything and everyone everywhere.

And crushing the last Archeron Crab like the goddamned insect it was. Its tough shell made an impression up through the deck, but it was a lot flatter than the creature had been only seconds before.

"Sweet Jovian Jesus," Inman breathed out, and lay right down on the deck next to the lump signifying the spot where the last Xeno was crushed.

"We did it!" Captain Mallory shouted from the cockpit.

"Bullshit," Sarge grumbled in the happy version of his grumble. "*You* did it, Captain."

"Well, okay," she said, "but you guys definitely helped."

We had come down close enough to the *resort* part of the resort planet that onlookers gathered to see what had happened. Those of us inside the *Tranquility* just waved at them in exhaustion.

"I like the way you work," Sarge told Mallory. "And, sad for me to say, we are in need of a new pilot. Ace was the best, so you'd have to be really good."

"Don't be a turd, sir," Dahlia said, and she laughed along with Sarge. "I think she might have passed the audition."

"We also need a ship," Sarge said. "Fix this one up, it might be right for some rebel scum on the run."

"You'll foot the bill, then?" Mallory asked with a smile.

"Naw, we'll just have Junebug jump up and down on the dent, it'll be good as new."

Mallory rested her forehead on the headrest of the copilot seat. "Great. It's hard enough for a pirate to make a living these days. And now we're taking on a bunch of smartasses."

Sarge looked at me and said, "Oh, Boz, I *like* this one. She's a ballbuster."

I almost said, *Takes one to know one*, but what the hell. "Maybe pass her a note in study hall, see if she *like* likes you."

"Damn, she's right. What a bunch of smartasses," he said with a shake of his head, then headed up front to talk to her.

THE END

CHECK OUT OTHER GREAT SCIENCE FICTION BOOKS

IN PERPETUITY
by Jake Bible

For two thousand years, Earth and her many colonies across the galaxy have fought against the Estelian menace. Having faced overwhelming losses, the CSC has instituted the largest military draft ever, conscripting millions into the battle against the aliens. Major Bartram North has been tasked with the unenviable task of coordinating the military education of hundreds of thousands of recruits and turning them into troops ready to fight and die for the cause.

As Major North struggles to maintain a training pace that the CSC insists upon, he realizes something isn't right on the Perpetuity. But before he can investigate, the station dissolves into madness brought on by the physical booster known as pharma. Unfortunately for Major North, that is not the only nightmare he faces- an armada of Estelian warships is on the edge of the solar system and headed right for Earth!

BATTLEFIELD MARS
by David Robbins

Several centuries into the future, Earth has established three colonies on Mars. No indigenous life has been discovered, and humankind looks forward to making the Red Planet their own.

Then 'something' emerges out of a long-extinct volcano and doesn't like what the humans are doing.

Captain Archard Rahn, United Nations Interplanetary Corps, tries to stem the rising tide of slaughter. But the Martians are more than they seem, and it isn't long before Mars erupts in all-out war.

SEVERED**PRESS**

f facebook.com/severedpress
◎ twitter.com/severedpress

CHECK OUT OTHER GREAT
SCIENCE FICTION BOOKS

MAUSOLEUM 2069
by Rick Jones

Political dignitaries including the President of the Federation gather for a ceremony onboard Mausoleum 2069. But when a cloud of interstellar dust passes through the galaxy and eclipses Earth, the tenants within the walls of Mausoleum 2069 are reborn and the undead begin to rise. As the struggle between life and death onboard the mausoleum develops, Eriq Wyman, a one-time member of a Special ops team called the Force Elite, is given the task to lead the President to the safety of Earth. But is Earth like Mausoleum 2069? A landscape of the living dead? Has the war of the Apocalypse finally begun? With so many questions there is only one certainty: in space there is nowhere to run and nowhere to hide.

RED CARBON
by D.J. Goodman

Diamonds have been discovered on Mars.

After years of neglect to space programs around the world, a ruthless corporation has made it to the Red Planet first, establishing their own mining operation with its own rules and laws, its own class system, and little oversight from Earth. Conditions are harsh, but its people have learned how to make the Martian colony home.

But something has gone catastrophically wrong on Earth. As the colony leaders try to cover it up, hacker Leah Hartnup is getting suspicious. Her boundless curiosity will lead her to a horrifying truth: they are cut off, possibly forever. There are no more supplies coming. There will be no more support. There is no more mission to accomplish. All that's left is one goal: survival.

CHECK OUT OTHER GREAT SCIENCE FICTION BOOKS

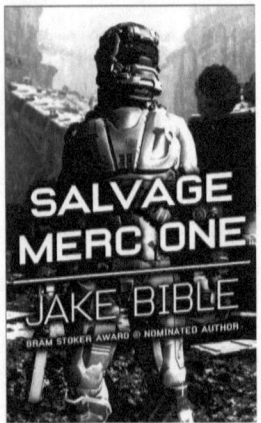

SALVAGE MERC ONE
by Jake Bible

Joseph Laribeau was born to be a Marine in the Galactic Fleet. He was born to fight the alien enemies known as the Skrang Alliance and travel the galaxy doing his duty as a Marine Sergeant. But when the War ended and Joe found himself medically discharged, the best job ever was over and he never thought he'd find his way again.

Then a beautiful alien walked into his life and offered him a chance at something even greater than the Fleet, a chance to serve with the Salvage Merc Corp.

Now known as Salvage Merc One Eighty-Four, Joe Laribeau is given the ultimate assignment by the SMC bosses. To his surprise it is neither a military nor a corporate salvage. Rather, Joe has to risk his life for one of his own. He has to find and bring back the legend that started the Corp.

SERENGETI
by J.B. Rockwell

It was supposed to be an easy job: find the Dark Star Revolution Starships, destroy them, and go home. But a booby-trapped vessel decimates the Meridian Alliance fleet, leaving Serengeti—a Valkyrie class warship with a sentient AI brain—on her own; wrecked and abandoned in an empty expanse of space. On the edge of total failure, Serengeti thinks only of her crew. She herds the survivors into a lifeboat, intending to sling them into space. But the escape pod sticks in her belly, locking the cryogenically frozen crew inside.

Then a scavenger ship arrives to pick Serengeti's bones clean. Her engines dead, her guns long silenced, Serengeti and her last two robots must find a way to fight the scavengers off and save the crew trapped inside her.

CHECK OUT OTHER GREAT SCIENCE FICTION BOOKS

FURNACE
by Joseph Williams

On a routine escort mission to a human colony, Lieutenant Michael Chalmers is pulled out of hyper-sleep a month early. The RSA Rockne Hummel is well off course and—as the ship's navigator—it's up to him to figure out why. It's supposed to be a simple fix, but when he attempts to identify their position in the known universe, nothing registers on his scans. The vessel has catapulted beyond the reach of starlight by at least a hundred trillion light-years. Then a planetary-mass object materializes behind them. It's burning brightly even without a star to heat it. Hundreds of damaged ships are locked in its orbit. The crew discovers there are no life-signs aboard any of them. As system failures sweep through the Hummel, neither Chalmers nor the pilot can prevent the vessel from crashing into the surface near a mysterious ancient city. And that's where the real nightmare begins.

LUNA
by Rick Chesler

On the threshold of opening the moon to tourist excursions, a private space firm owned by a visionary billionaire takes a team of non-astronauts to the lunar surface. To address concerns that the moon's barren rock may not hold long-term allure for an uber-wealthy clientele, the company's charismatic owner reveals to the group the ultimate discovery: life on the moon.

But what is initially a triumphant and world-changing moment soon gives way to unrelenting terror as the team experiences firsthand that despite their technological prowess, the moon still holds many secrets.